The VERY REAL
Ghost Book
of Christina Rose

The VERY REAL *Ghost Book* of Christina Rose

From the Not-So-Private Files of Ghost Hunters I.N.K.

James M. Deem

A Yearling Book

Published by
Bantam Doubleday Dell Books for Young Readers
a division of
Bantam Doubleday Dell Publishing Group, Inc.
1540 Broadway
New York, New York 10036

Visit us on the Web! www.bdd.com

Educators and librarians, visit the BDD Teacher's Resource Center at www.bdd.com/teachers

ISBN: 0-440-41426-1

Reprinted by arrangement with Houghton Mifflin Company

Printed in the United States of America

October 1998

10 9 8 7 6 5 4 3 2

OPM

For my very own
B.F.M.A.s and B.O.M.A.s

Chloe, David
Rachel, Anna

Everything in this book is true and really happened as I described it.*

Signed: *Christina Rose*

---

*And if you don't believe me, my brother Danny and our friend Roberto Wing also know about most of the things that happened, so this is their ghost book, too. It's just that I'm the writer, Danny's the artist, and Roberto's the comedian.**

**Don't you like ***s? I like how they look and how they act. They make it seem like there's secret information at the bottom of the page (even if there's not).

Remember Me

by Christina Rossetti

Remember me when I am gone away,
   Gone far away into the silent land;
   When you can no more hold me by the hand,
Nor I half turn to go yet turning stay.
Remember me when no more day by day
   You tell me of your future that you planned:
   Only remember me; you understand
It will be late to counsel then or pray.
Yet if you should forget me for a while
   And afterwards remember, do not grieve:
   For if the darkness and corruption leave
   A vestige of the thoughts that once I had,
Better by far you should forget and smile
   Than that you should remember and be sad.

Introduction

by Professor I. Barrymore
Associate Professor, Mid-Coastal California College,
Oro del Mar, California

I have been asked by Christina Rose to introduce her very first book of ghosts, with illustrations by Dante Rose and additional humor by Roberto Wing. I shall gladly do so by describing what happened the first time Christina visited my home and began to scan the shelves of my rather large collection of books regarding the paranormal.

She picked up *Lord Halifax's Ghost Book*, a rather dog-eared tome published quite a long time ago and filled with some rather dubious ghost stories.

As she perused its pages she said as I recall, "This looks like a nice fat book of ghosts."

That, dear readers, sums up precisely what you are now holding in your hands, except that it is an even nicer and an even fatter book of ghosts. And, why shouldn't it be? It's *The VERY REAL Ghost Book of Christina Rose*.

Contents

1. My Very First Ghost   1

2. Another Plane Crash   15

3. Ghost Radar   25

4. The Widow and Mr. Hans Hanson   36

5. Ghosts in the Attic   53

6. A Tricky Ghost   62

7. Onward and Upward   74

8. The Phantom Apple Crisp   83

9. The Ghosts of Rossetti and Rose   93

10. The Investigation Continues   106

11. Christina's Reading   121

12. The California Poltergeist   133

13. The Very Last Ghost Story—Not!   151

1
My Very First Ghost

My name is Christina Rose and I believe in ghosts.

Not all those fake scary movie ghosts or book ghosts with cleavers and chainsaws and waxy dead eyes, but regular REAL ghosts. The kind that just watch you from the corners of your room. The kind that wait until you catch a glimpse of them. The kind that are lonely and miss you and just want to be loved.

Please don't start thinking that I'm crazy or weird. I never would have written any of this three weeks ago because I didn't think that ghosts were anybody's business—except my own. It's just that we moved, and a few things happened in our new house in our new town. A few things that got me to change my mind.

Professor Barrymore said to write it all down, so everyone could know about my very own poltergeist.

But I can't just start with that story. Ghosts are much more complicated than that. I have to start at the beginning, a long time ago, with another ghost story. A *real* ghost story.

My Very First Ghost Story

Two people from New York City fall in love and get married. They have two children, and the woman quits her job and devotes all her time to her young family. She loves her children very much and, for three years, spends every day with them.

One day her college roommate who lives in Maine calls and asks her to visit for a long weekend. At first the woman says no, but her husband convinces her that a short vacation would be fun. Reluctantly, she agrees.

At LaGuardia Airport, on the day of her flight, the woman wants to change her mind. She looks at the faces of her children and thinks she will miss them too much. But her husband has planned a special surprise. He gives the children a small box wrapped in shiny paper and tells them to hand it to their mother. In it she finds a silver heart-shaped locket with a picture of each child inside as a goodbye present. Engraved twice, once on the front and once on the back, are the words "Remember Me."

"Wear this so you won't feel lonely," her husband tells her.

"This is so sweet," the mother says, putting it around her neck. She is crying, but she is happy. "But you make me feel so thoughtless. I should have bought the kids a present, too."

"Don't worry," he says, "I can get them something. And they'll have me if they start to miss you. Have a great time."

She kisses everyone goodbye and gets on board. On the way, a terrible thunderstorm surrounds the plane. Lightning hits the cockpit and the controls are damaged. The plane begins to lose too much altitude and crashes in the woods outside Bangor. The woman and all the passengers die.

The father hears about the crash after his children are asleep that night. He is sick with grief, but he decides not to wake them. In the morning, when he enters their room, the children are already awake. They are talking to each other and playing with their dog.

"Momma came home last night," the girl says.

"No, she didn't," the father replies, his heart breaking.

"She did, too," the girl says. Then she holds up the Remember Me locket in her hand.

"Where did you get that?" the father asks, taking the locket.

"Momma gave it to me," she says. "Can I wear it when I grow up?"

"Your mother wasn't here," the father says, putting it in his pocket. "She was in an airplane." Then he tells them about the crash.

The children begin to cry.

That day, friends and relatives crowd the house. The boy and girl eat chocolate cake and sugar cookies and drink a lot of soda, like they're at a party. Only it doesn't feel like a party. The girl hears everyone talk about her mother's death. She tries to say that her mother visited her the night before and brought her the Remember Me locket, but no one pays any attention.

At bedtime the father tells them they will bury their mother soon.

"Where is Momma?" the girl asks.

"Where the plane crashed," the father says.

"Why can't she come here?" she asks.

"She can't, honey."

"Why not?"

"Because she's dead."

Then the father kisses them goodnight and starts to leave the room.

"But I saw Momma," the girl tries to explain. "She left her locket for me."

"You had a dream about your mother," the father says. "And you got confused. The locket must have fallen off your mom's neck when she hugged you goodbye," he tells her. "Remember? You were wearing your raincoat and it has such big pockets. I bet it dropped into your pocket, and that's where you found it. Stranger things have happened, you know, so please don't go making anything scary out of this. There's no such thing as a ghost."

"Ghost?" the brother says. The word startles him. Only now does he realize that his sister must have seen their mother's ghost.

The girl reacts differently.

Ghost? (she thinks) *My mother didn't look*

like a ghost. She wasn't scary. But she didn't look like a dream. She looked real. And she gave me her locket.

None of them knew or understood what had happened. And they never discussed it again—at least for a long time.

That is where this story ends. It is the saddest ghost story I know, because it is real.

VERY REAL.

Okay, the woman is my mom, Judith Rose. She died in a plane crash when my brother Dante (call him Danny, if you value your life) and I were three. At first I thought I really saw her the night she died. I thought I was awake when I saw her come into the room. She walked to Danny's bed and looked at him. That night he was sleeping with Sparky, our West Highland white terrier, because Danny missed Mom so much.

A second later, my mother glanced at me and saw me watching her. She came to my bed and smiled and put her finger to her lips and then patted my covers. I closed my eyes and fell asleep. In the morning I found the locket on my bed and my dad took it. Super-smart computer software writer that he is, he was determined to make me believe that it was just a dream. He made his speech, trying to convince me, but inside I knew he was wrong. Inside, I knew I was not supposed to talk about it.

Danny was another story. The next year, when we got separate bedrooms, he started thinking that every looming shadow and every strange noise after sundown was a ghost coming to get him. He must have thought they were blood-dripping, night-creeping, life-sucking monsters or something. He checked under his bed and in his closet every night. And he slept with his light on until fourth grade. He would never say it (Danny isn't the talkative type), but I knew what he was thinking: *What if Mom misses us too much? What if she comes back for us? What if she wants to take us with her?*

Danny went crazy about ghosts (and I mean CRAZY) for a long time. Then the second part happened.

My Very First Ghost Story (continued)

For a long time afterward, the girl wonders about ghosts. She wonders whether she will ever see her mother's ghost again, either in a dream or in real life. She wonders whether her father will give her the Remember Me locket one day, and she wonders how she got it in the first place.

Her father can tell she is wondering too

much, so he tries to distract her. He gives her lots of girl toys—Barbies and blond baby dolls. But she dresses them in black and colors their hair with black (and sometimes blue) Magic Marker.

So her father gives her a computer with lots of fun software. The girl likes her computer and learns the alphabet and shapes from it, but still she wonders. Then her father teaches her to read and gives her books about ballerinas and ice skaters.

Nothing seems to work, until her sixth birthday when her father gives her a pet mouse. She calls it Mousie, and it becomes her best friend for almost one year. Then Mousie dies. The girl decides to bury him in the back yard. She dresses in black and cuts a pair of tights to use as a veil. She even dresses her dog in a black bow for the ceremony.

"What are you doing?" her father asks.

She is carrying a small box that holds Mousie.

"Let me see," her father says, lifting the lid and looking at Mousie's body. "What's this?"

"His locket," the girl answers. She has made a necklace with a heart-shaped pendant from aluminum foil and placed it around Mousie's neck.

She sees that her father is upset, so she hurries out the door. With her dog's help, she digs a hole under a lilac bush and buries the box.

That night, after she goes to bed, she gets a funny feeling. She gets up and looks out her back window. There, standing by Mousie's grave, is a shadowy figure. She watches a moment until the figure walks into the deeper darkness by the side of the house. She is certain that her mother's ghost has come to visit Mousie. But she doesn't tell anyone. She knows she cannot tell her brother because ghosts frighten him too much. And she knows that she cannot tell her father because he does not believe in ghosts.

Every night for a week (and after that as often as she can), the girl looks out the window in hopes of catching another glimpse of her mother's ghost. She hates to fall asleep, and so she tries to stay awake as long as she can.

Her father gives her another pet, this time a goldfish. She thinks that if the goldfish dies and is buried in the back yard her mother's ghost will come to visit again. She doesn't change the goldfish's water and forgets to feed it. But when the goldfish dies and she buries it next to Mousie, her mother's ghost never visits.

She finds dead insects and buries them as well. Soon a whole corner of the backyard is her special cemetery. But her mother's ghost never visits.

She grows up, loving to write on her computer. She writes a computer diary filled with her regular thoughts and her ghosty thoughts. She writes poems and stories and saves them on her disks. One day she finds a book of poetry that her mother liked. In it she discovers a special poem. She types it into her computer diary and then memorizes part of it and recites it to herself when she thinks about her mother:

I rose at the dead of night
And went to the lattice alone
To look for my Mother's ghost
Where the ghostly moonlight shone.

My Mother raised her eyes,
They were blank and could not see;
Yet they held me with their stare
While they seemed to look at me.

She opened her mouth and spoke,
I could not hear a word
While my flesh crept on my bones
And every hair was stirred.

I strained to catch her words
And she strained to make me hear,
But never a sound of words
Fell on my straining ear.

But no matter how many times she watches from her window in the middle of the night, whispering her poem like a prayer, nothing else happens. . . .

Okay, my father always said I had a flair for the dramatic, but that doesn't mean I'm making any of this up. Mousie was real, but so was what I saw from my bedroom window.

Maybe you'd think that way too if you were named for your mother's favorite poet: Christina G-word Rossetti. Her middle name and mine are the same, but you'll never catch me writing it here (and if you think you're so smart and go look it up somewhere, don't make any jokes about it, *please!*). My mother loved her poetry *so* much, too much probably, if you think about her giving me that particular G-word for a middle name. Christina G-word Rossetti thought a lot about ghosts and wrote *ghosty* poems, and so do I, Christina G-word Rose. Only I never wrote anything for anyone to read until now.

If I was a ghost story writer, I could make up really interesting and scary endings to my stories. I mean, my first two ghost stories just kind of stop. Nothing happens. I mean, *nothing happens!* They don't have scary endings that make your skin crawl. But give my stories to some stupid ghost story writers and they'd change them all around. They'd make my mother's ghost all *burned* and *bloody* with her skull showing through. And she'd hold out her bony skeleton arms with tattered clothes and flesh hanging from them, calling to her children.

DAAAAANNNNNNNY, CHRIIIISTIIIIINA!
COME WITH MEEEEEEEE!
WOOO! WOOO! WOOOOOOO!

And the room would be dark and the windows would be open and the wind would be howling and long filmy curtains would be blowing. The ghost, with a wild gleam in its eyes, would float toward the window, beckoning to the children, and suddenly their father would come into the room and watch in horror as they stood on the windowsill—ready to die—and he would grab them by their nightclothes and save them one split second from certain death in the fish pond three stories below.

Gross! Now, do you understand why ghosts never scared me? Ghosts didn't act like that—they acted like my mother's ghost, if she was a ghost. They were quiet. They were shy. You couldn't really tell if they were ghosts or dreams. They never ever came back even if you really wanted them to. And you didn't talk about them with anybody—especially your dad—because *nobody* would believe you.

But that was three weeks ago. It's funny how much life can change in such a short time. If you had told me then that I would now be the president of Ghost Hunters I.N.K. ("We Investigate All Hauntings"), I would have said "You're crazy." And if you had said that I would wrestle with my very own poltergeist, I would have said, "You're seriously crazy!"

Now I have more stories to tell. Some are my ghost stories, some are other people's. When I'm done, you'll know what happened. When I'm done, you'll know what's real. And when you're done, you'll have one book of *very real* ghosts staring you dead in the face.

And believe me, you won't be dreaming either.

2

Another Plane Crash

"Presents!" Dad yelled one day last spring. Actually, it wasn't just any old day. It was April fourteenth, I remember very well, the anniversary of another major tragedy: the day the *Titanic* sank.

"Open yours first, Christina," he said, handing me two boxes. Inside a Bloomingdale's box I found a Flapdoodles top with bike shorts. Both were *pink!* In the second box was a bike helmet with pink and turquoise racing stripes, and a handwritten coupon:

"What are these pink things for?" I didn't get it. Larchmont had too many hills and too much traffic for bike riding—and I wasn't about to do anything in pink anyway. Dad knew that.

"Just a minute," he said. "Okay, Danny, it's your turn."

Danny had one huge box, big enough to hold an industrial-size ironing board.

"What is it?" he asked a moment later, staring at a piece of fluorescent green wood.

"A surfboard," Dad said. "Now, read this."

Then he handed us a greeting card he had made on his computer. The front showed a seagull flying over a beach on a sunny day. Inside was a little poem:

> My heart is like a singing bird
> Whose nest is in a watered shoot;
> My heart is like an apple tree
> Whose boughs are bent with thickset fruit;
> My heart is like a rainbow shell
> That paddles in a halcyon sea;
> My heart is gladder than all these
> Because . . .
> I got a job!

"You got a job?" Danny asked, sounding like Dad had just contracted chicken pox.

"Don't say it like that," Dad said. "Yes, I got a job!

Isn't that great? We're moving to California, land of computer opportunity and sunshine. Land of new bikes and water for surfing."

This was great news for Dad. After Mom died, he had stopped working to take care of us. He used the insurance money and stayed home. He baked cookies and cakes and made our Halloween costumes. He took us to school and picked us up. He coached my soccer team and was room parent every year. He made sure that Danny and I had normal lives —and we did, living twenty miles north of New York City in Larchmont, going to Weaver Street School.

I remember what he told us next: "There will be sunny beaches, palm trees, and blue skies. You'll have Rollerblades and skateboards. You can wear shorts all year long and maybe one year we can afford to build a swimming pool in our back yard. And best of all, I'll be gainfully employed, and we'll be living someplace new, away from all this—"

That's where he stopped talking, but it was easy to fill in the blank. *Sadness*, he was thinking, *all this sadness*. Everyone at school knew that we were "the kids whose mother died in that awful plane crash." It *was* hard to listen to that seven years after the accident. And every time Grandma and Grandpa saw us, they got *that look* in their eyes.

"Your mother's hair was just this color in the sunlight," Grandma would say, stroking my hair. I loved

Grandma, but it made me cringe—especially the older I got.

If I thought about that part of our lives, moving was okay. But moving wasn't okay when I thought about leaving my best friends, Alison and Jeanne, or my school, or our house, or. . . .

"Nooo!" I screamed at Dad. I ran up to my room and slammed the door. Then I kicked my soccer ball against the wall. I wanted to knock it right into the back yard.

Dad opened the door and walked in.

"You didn't knock," I said.

"You're going to break something."

"I don't want to live anywhere else."

"I know you don't want to," he said. "But it's time."

"For you maybe, but not for me."

"For all of us," he said. "It's like we've been living with your mom for the last seven years. I need to make some changes now. I need to have my own life—with you and Danny—away from here."

"Why can't you have a new life here?"

"Because there's too much of your mother around here, and the jobs aren't good around here, and it costs too much. We need some money coming in or you and Danny aren't going to college. Do you know

what our property taxes are? I don't want to do anything that would make you sad, but taking this job
and moving to California is something that will be
good for us. Really. Hey, you know, life is full of surprises, and they don't always have to be bad ones."

"Well, I WON'T fly," I warned him. "So don't
even think about it!"

"We're driving," Dad reassured me.

Danny was much easier than me. "Cool," he said,
sounding like some surf dude. At least, that's how he
sounded at first.

That night I had a dream, a *ghosty* dream:

A Ghosty Dream

It is evening and I am on an airplane. As I
dream about the plane, I (the dream girl) realize I have dreamed about the same airplane
many times. That's when it flies into a dangerous thunderstorm. The plane bounces and
jerks around like a marionette, and the pilot is
having trouble controlling it. The passengers
are buckled into their seats, perspiring like
crazy, trying not to think about the possibilities. The voice of the flight attendant comes
over the intercom and tells everyone, "The
pilot needs someone to help fly the plane."

Even though everyone is scared that the plane will crash, no one volunteers—except the dream girl, the girl whose mother died.

She makes her way to the cockpit. The pilot, a grandfatherly man with white hair, asks her to sit in the copilot's seat. As she steps forward, she notices someone standing beside the empty seat. It's not the copilot, it's . . . it's the ghost of her mother. She looks beautiful, just like in her pictures, only she's crying. At first the dream girl thinks they are tears of happiness. The ghost is holding the Remember Me locket, which the dream girl hasn't seen since she was three, and as the girl sits in the copilot's chair, her mother's ghost places the locket around her neck.

"I want you to have the locket," the ghost says, still crying.

"I will wear it forever," the girl says.

"I brought it to you before. Your father should have given it to you, but now it is too late. Too late."

Then the girl realizes why the ghost is not happy that she's finally seeing her daughter again; she's sad because she knows that the plane is going to crash, that there's nothing she can do to help her daughter. The locket cannot save her either. The daughter is very brave and tries to help the pilot, but the plane goes into a deadly tailspin. Then the mother's ghost wraps her arms around the daughter and holds her for the last few moments before. . . .

That's when I woke up and realized I had seen my mother's ghost a third time. Okay, yes, I know it was a dream, but I believe that ghosts can visit your dreams. It wasn't like I dreamed about her every night or even once a year. So when I woke up, I couldn't help myself. I looked for the locket even though I knew Dad had it.

It wasn't there.

Weird, I thought. *Why did I have this dream? Did my mother want to tell me something? Did she want me to have the locket?*

The next morning I considered telling my father about the dream, but I couldn't. He would just think I was being weird (as usual). So I did something equally weird.

"Can I have Mom's locket?" I asked.

"What?"

"You know, her locket? Remember Me?"

"What about it?"

"Can I have it?" I repeated. He was making this so hard.

"Maybe," he said. "One day."

"Where is it? Can I see it at least?"

"It's put away."

"When can I have it?"

"I don't want to talk about it now."

"You know, Mom doesn't want us to move," I told him.

"What makes you say that?"

"I had a dream last night. I'm sure Mom doesn't want us to move. She was in my dream."

"Christina!" He was very annoyed. "How can you say that? Why would she want you to stay here? Maybe *you* want to stay here, but that has nothing to do with your mother. So, please, stop arguing with me. Just help me. This isn't going to be easy for any of us, you know."

I stopped arguing, but I never really liked the idea. We had to clean the attic and basement and all of the closets. And we had to throw out lots of stuff. I found a pair of sunglasses that belonged to my mom. Dad was ready to dump them, but I said no. How could I throw her sunglasses out even if they were scratched? And how could we leave the only place that reminded me of her? At least I could wear her sunglasses in California.

Since Dad wasn't about to change his mind, I made up for it in other ways. I got him to take me on a final shopping trip to Bloomingdale's. I bought lots of black things: black jeans, black T-shirts, black boots. No Flapdoodles. And I made him agree to a bunch of farewell slumber parties with Alison and Jeanne. We all promised we would be friends forever and write every week. Everyone thought it was great that I'd get to live in California with all those palm trees and beaches and sunny afternoons. I just smiled and thought about bleak winter days with frosty wind and snow on snow and ghosty figures silhouetted against gray skies.

Of course, Dad didn't mention *everything* about California: the smog, the fog, the big bugs, and the guys who get tattoos all over their body (even their shaved heads) and then go to the beach to show off.

And he forgot three of the really important things:

1.   North Klondike, our new town, was a *very* strange place.

2.   We would be buying an old *pink* house. (If he couldn't get me to wear pink clothes, he must have thought he could get me to live in a pink house.)

3.   Not that it was important, but the pink house was *haunted*. (Only I didn't know it then.)

But, hey, as Dad might have said, life is full of little surprises. And sometimes you can't tell if they are good or bad—or *scary*!

3

Ghost Radar

I have always thought I had Ghost Radar. Why else would I have woken up to see my mother the night she died or watched her standing by Mousie's grave? It was working when we left New York near the end of July, pulling our U-Haul trailer, and it should have been working when we arrived at North Klondike, only it wasn't. The place was *so* strange that it threw my Ghost Radar out of whack. It was *so* strange you would have thought we moved to Oz instead of California. The day we got there we were driving down Ocean Breeze Way—our new street—heading for our pink house. When Dad first told us the street name, it made me think of a sandy beach and sea gulls and waves lulling me to sleep. He never told us that the beach was ten miles away and full of rocks.

That was the first strange thing about North Klondike. It's a small town *almost* on the coast, either about four hours or four days north of L.A., depending on the traffic. There isn't a South Klondike or an East Klondike or a West Klondike, unless it's in the Pacific Ocean. And if you want to know the truth, there wasn't even supposed to be a North Klondike, only a Klondike, except Mr. Nebuchadnezzar Klondike (the founding father) made a mistake when he filled out all the paperwork.*

Even after one hundred years, North Klondike is still so small that you won't find it on some maps. It has five restaurants (if you count the AM/PM Mini Mart as one), two small grocery stores, one hardware/drug store with a post office, one tiny part-time library, an ATM, and fifteen gas stations (okay, this *is* California!). There is also one California-type store (the Klondike Krystal Palace) that sells incense, crystals, New Age books, muffins, cookies, and Snapple, and maybe a few other places, but if you want to go to the movies or buy groceries in a regular supermarket, you have to drive up the coast to Oro del Mar. If you

---

*This is no secret. Back in 1887, Mr. Nebuchadnezzar Klondike (who hated his first name and probably his parents, too) wanted to create his own paradise, so he decided to build a town and name it for himself: Klondike. But when it came time to write the town name on the form, he wrote N. Klondike and the dumb people in Sacramento thought he meant North Klondike (when he was really just signing his own name, N. Klondike) and that's how the town got its name. It really didn't matter what he called it, because there wasn't enough water and not enough people moved to N. Klondike anyway. If you don't believe this, you will have to ask Roberto Wing. He swears it's true.

want to go to a mall, you have to drive even farther—
all the way to San Luis Obispo. And if you want to go
swimming, well, by now you know that you need
to drive, and if you don't drive, well . . . you need to
pedal a lot—but not wearing a *pink* bike helmet!

—∾∾—

The second strange thing was our new neighborhood. As we drove down Ocean Breeze Way, I saw
lots of palm trees—and a dead end. Out here, they
call it a *cul-de-sac*. On one side are the old run-down
Victorian houses that were built when Mr. Klondike
was alive. On the other side are seven almost new
ranch homes that look alike (except for the color of
the front doors). They were supposed to be part of a
big new subdivision, but it went broke. Our house is
at the very end, beside a really rundown Victorian
and across from a ranch house with a yellow door.

All I can say is that it didn't look like Larchmont—or the California of anybody's dreams.

The neighborhood was even stranger, though. As soon as Dad pulled the U-Haul into the driveway, I looked over and saw a sign on the yellow-door neighbors' front lawn:

MME. OLGA

PSYCHIC

MOST EVENINGS, BY APPOINTMENT ONLY

The last line gave her psychic hotline number.*

Welcome to California, Dad, Land of Computer and Psychic Opportunity!

"Well, what do you think?" Dad asked as he unlocked the rear of the U-Haul.

"Why did you buy this place?" I asked.

"Because it's a Victorian. I've always wanted a Victorian house. Did you notice," he said, pointing to the roof, "that it's got a little gingerbread work on it? See the white trim under the eaves?"

"It looks like a cartoon house," I complained. "Is this where Mickey and Minnie used to live before Disneyland?"

---

*I'm sorry Mme. Olga, but I pictured you with green hair, dangly eyeball earrings, long black fingernails, a huge wart on your chin, and a crystal around your neck. What did I know, right?

"Come on, Christina," Dad said.

"But it's on a dead end and we're living across from a psychic."

"Oh, Carol is nice."

"Carol?"

"That's Mme. Olga's real name. Actually, it's Carolina Olga Medina Wing."

"How do you know she has a real name?" I asked.

"I met her the day I signed the papers on the house. She had me over for dinner."

"Did she tell your future?" I asked. "Like that we're moving back to New York?"

"No," he explained. "You know what I think about that kind of stuff. She owns the Klondike Krystal Palace, so she must do the psychic stuff for fun. Anyway, you and Danny will like her. And she has a son your age named Roberto. You'll all be in sixth grade."

Just then Danny slammed the car door so hard that the U-Haul shook. "I want Sparky back," he said angrily. He had changed his mind about moving to California as soon as he found out that Sparky wasn't coming with us. By now he hated the idea of leaving New York even more than I did.

"Danny, for the very last time, Sparky's staying in New York," Dad told him. "And that's all there is to it."

"But it's not fair!"

The absolute worst part about moving to California was not our new neighborhood or the weird town or even our pink house. It was moving without Sparky, who would have won the Westie championship for the perkiest ears and pointiest tail and yappiest yip.

Actually, Sparky had been Mom's dog, but after Mom died, Danny claimed him. It was complicated growing up without a mother, and Sparky helped. Whenever we were feeling sad, Sparky was a great person to cuddle with. Yes, I know I wrote *person*. I know Sparky wasn't a person, but that's how he seemed—especially to Danny. When something's bothering me, I can usually read or write in my diary or kick a soccer ball or even hibernate in my room and forget about it. But Danny needed Sparky.

All that changed when Dad decided that Sparky would be better off staying in New York. Dad said that Sparky was too old and wouldn't adjust well. So he gave Sparky to Grandma and Grandpa right before we left. Now that we didn't have him, Danny was sadder than I had ever seen him. And I wasn't feeling much happier.

"We just got here," Dad said. "We fought about this the whole way. Can't we stop fighting? Sparky couldn't make the trip. He's too old. Okay? Do you think I wanted to leave him in New York? It would've been a lot easier to bring him with us. But it wasn't possible."

Welcome to California, Dad, happy home of the gainfully employed and unhappy home of the dogless!

You probably think I'm being too dramatic again. I mean, so what if the town has a weird name or if a psychic lives next door? I could ignore those if nothing else strange was going on. *But that wasn't all!* Two really strange things happened.

The first took place after Dad gave us on a tour of our new house. Hippies used to live there, he said. *Hippies who didn't know how to paint,* I was thinking.

The house needed a paint job outside, and not just because it was bright pink. The paint was peeling and the wood looked a little spongy in spots. Inside, the house was a real jewel: the living room was turquoise, the kitchen was emerald green, and the only bathroom was ruby red with a glitter globe light. It also had an old rust-stained tub and no shower—really gross! All the windows were the original ones, which meant they had been painted so many times that they couldn't be opened. That didn't matter because some of them had broken panes; you could just take off the taped-on cardboard and let the air in.

"Don't worry," Dad said, when we stopped in my room, "we're going to fix it up."

At least my room was big, with high ceilings, lots of sunlight, and the grossest flowery wallpaper, although most of it was peeling.

"I know, I know," he said. "We'll go to the store and get some different wallpaper and paint. I already hired someone to redo the bathroom."

"But what about the kitchen?" I asked. "It's really disgusting."

"New appliances are being delivered this afternoon. And I'll paint it and maybe redo the cabinet fronts. It'll be okay. Really."

"I thought everything was new in California," Danny said.

"Not everything," Dad said. "But we have a new life here. Doesn't that count for something?"

Danny and I looked at each other. "No," we agreed.

"Anyway, I want you to have this," Dad said.

"What?" Danny asked.

"Look," Dad said, opening his hand in front of me. He was holding the Remember Me locket. I hadn't seen it since I was three, but I recognized it immediately. "I was going to save it till you were older, but this seems like a good time: a new place, a new life, a special memory."

He handed me the locket, and . . . well, I dropped it. It was weird. I *swear* I got an electric shock. I would never have dropped it otherwise. I'm not clumsy—I made the travel team in soccer two years in a row. But there it was on the floor.

"Christina, you've got to be careful with this," Dad said, picking it up.

"I was being careful," I argued. "I got a shock from it."

"Look, it's very special. I'll keep it if you don't want it. Maybe you aren't ready for this."

"Fine," I said. "I'm a baby."

I burst out crying.

Danny was standing there like he wished I would stop, and Dad was feeling guilty.

"It's okay," he said. "It's okay. You keep the locket. You are old enough. I'm sorry." And he slipped it over my head. "Now, look inside."

I popped the catch. Inside were two tiny pictures of my mother: the first one my father had ever taken of her—in London where they had met on a vacation—and the last one we had. Dad had taken it at the airport the night she flew away.

I hugged Dad and kept crying. By then Danny had disappeared.

The other strange thing waited until the next morning.

Dad was downstairs making his organic oatmeal pancakes on our new stove. Before you make a rash judgment, Dad's pancakes are really tasty—even if they are almost 99% nutritious. It's one of our favorite breakfasts (even Sparky used to like them), and definitely worth hurrying for.

I was in my room, brushing my hair, trying to get downstairs in a hurry, when Danny walked in.

"Rrrrrready for pancakes?" I asked, then wished I hadn't. That was what we said to Sparky before we gave him a bite.

Danny didn't say anything, but his face looked like it was ready to crack into a thousand pieces. I knew what he was thinking.

"I miss Sparky, too," I said, trying to make Danny feel better. "But you know Grandma and Grandpa are taking good care of him."

"Don't talk about him." Danny sounded pretty angry. "He's my dog, and it's just not fair."

"Come on," I said, putting my brush down, "let's go eat. We can ask Dad for a fish tank."

Just then my hairbrush flipped up into the air and, well, sort of flew (that's what it looked like) behind the dresser. I wasn't sure then what had happened because I wasn't paying that much attention. I was thinking more about Danny.

"Did you see that?" I asked Danny.

"Yeah. You must have hit it with your hand."

Then Dad called from the kitchen, "Your pancakes are getting cold!"

Danny headed for the stairs. I got down on my hands and knees and reached behind the dresser for the brush. I was thinking: *Maybe my hand bumped the brush.*

Or maybe not.

Whatever had happened, it was one more strange thing about North Klondike.

If my Ghost Radar hadn't been short-circuited by this weird place, I might have realized what was happening. Unfortunately, the word *ghost* never even entered my mind. But that was before we met Roberto Wing, son of Mme. Olga the psychic, who pushed the reset button on my radar in no time flat.

4

The Widow and Mr. Hans Hanson

Early the next morning we drove to Oro del Mar to return the U-Haul. All of us were in a bad mood. Too much unpacking and too little sleep.

"Hey look," Dad said afterwards as we drove past some stores in the Oro del Mar-kette Shopping Center. "That place sells bagels."

"Where?" I asked. All I saw was a surf shop and an antique store.

"There," Dad said, quickly turning into the parking lot. "Pacific Waves. See the sign? It's a bagel place. Let's get some. That'll cheer us up."

"Get poppy seed!" I ordered.

"And sesame," Danny added. "And no plain."

"And some good cream cheese, too!"

Bagels were what New York was about for us: a basket full of toasted, seeded bagels with a big dish of chive cream cheese for smearing on top. As Dad walked into the store, I was thinking: *Maybe California won't be so bad if we have bagels.*

It wasn't Dad's fault, but *Pacific Waves* was a wipe-out. When he got in the car, he had a funny look on his face.

"They didn't exactly have poppy seed," he told me.

"Then I'll take sesame."

"Me too," Danny said.

"Didn't have that," he said, reaching into the bag. "They had chocolate chip and, let's see, here's taco."

"A taco bagel? That's disgusting!"

"Well, how about blueberry or strawberry? Or what about one called 'morning sunshine'? I think it's got orange juice, wheat germ, and sunflower seeds in it."

"Oh, gross," Danny said.

"Those aren't real bagels," I protested.

"They're Oro del Mar bagels," Dad said.

"You mean, Oro del Barf," Danny complained.

"Whatever you call them, I've got a dozen. Come on, try a blueberry," he said, handing me one. "It can't be so bad. You like blueberries."

I squished it between my fingers.

"This looks like blue Wonder Bread!"

"Maybe it's better with a little cream cheese," he suggested.

"Chive cream cheese on a blueberry bagel?"

"No, they didn't have anything *normal* like that. They had walnut raisin cream cheese. I got a little container of that. Or some honey sesame. That might be okay."

"I can't eat this," I said, handing him the "bagel."

"Neither can I," Dad admitted. "Maybe we can feed them to the seagulls."

At home, we unpacked some more. Then we had a quiet lunch of canned tuna and plain white bread. Afterwards Danny and I headed outside—and ran right into a big blob of loneliness.

Sometimes being lonely isn't so bad. I can kind of disappear for a while until I feel better. But it's bad when Danny and I both feel lonely. With just one look, we know what the other is feeling: there's nothing to do and no one to do it with.

"Want to play soccer?" he asked that afternoon, out of desperation. We hadn't played soccer together in years.

"Sure," I said, desperate myself.

Boys are *terrible* soccer players, don't you think? They won't use teamwork, they want to be stars and make all the goals. I stopped playing soccer with Danny a long time ago. Sometimes he kicked the ball too hard, and sometimes, if he was feeling wild, he aimed it at me. But what else was there to do? We had three weeks till school started, and nothing in the world to do.

It was not the kind of California day Dad had promised. A marine layer had settled in. It was sunny and hot everywhere else in the state, but it was foggy, cold, and damp along the coast, even if the coast was ten miles away. I didn't care. I was wearing Mom's sunglasses anyway.

The weather just made everything worse. I had even thought about checking some books out of the North Klondike Library, but, thanks to the town budget, it was closed ("Open Fridays Only, 10:00 A.M. to 4:00 P.M. NO FUNDS!").

So Danny and I kicked the soccer ball around.

Of course, the worst kind of loneliness happened accidentally—and ALWAYS when other people were around. Like when a boy with straight black hair and wire-rimmed glasses walked over from Mme. Olga's ranch house and introduced himself as Roberto Wing. We started to introduce ourselves, but he stopped us.

"I know," he said. "My mom told me. She said to bring over these cookies and say hi. Is your mom home?"

Danny and I just looked at him.

"You want me to give these to your mom?" he asked again.

Danny wasn't about to say anything (he *never* talked about Mom) so I opened my mouth and said, "Our mom is dead, we live with our dad. Thanks for the cookies."

I took the plate covered in aluminum foil.

"I just live with my mom," Roberto said, looking kind of sad himself. "My mom and dad split up, and now I've got a split personality. Half of it's here and the other half is in San Jose."

"Why San Jose?" San Jose was four hours up the coast.

"That's where my father lives," Roberto said. "Kind of. I mean, if you can call it living. You might call it something else. Sometimes I do. Like, *totally tubular, dude!*"

Roberto Wing was definitely strange himself.

"This is Widow Hanson's house, you know."

I looked at Danny. "I thought we bought it from the Mazzas."

"We did."

"I don't mean that," Roberto explained. "Widow Hanson died in 1950. She hasn't been around for a long time. I mean, not exactly around."

"What do you mean?" I asked.

"Don't you know that everybody in town calls this the Ghost House?"

"What?"

"Widow Hanson and her husband, Hans, lived in this house. Only she wasn't Widow Hanson when Hans was alive. But she's Widow Hanson now."

"No," I corrected. "She's dead now."

"She's not exactly dead either," Roberto said. "Her ghost walks the halls of your house. I guess she was just *dying* to be a ghost! And I've seen her. Standing in the front attic window. She's all white and see-through, like she's made out of curtains or something. And she's really ugly and old and very scary. And I don't know how you can live in the house and not know she's there."

"That's not true," I said. "Have you looked at our attic windows? They're boarded up."

"It is too true," Roberto said. "At night the boards disappear and Widow Hanson stands there. I ought to know. I live across the street. Do you want to hear how she turned into a ghost?"

What would you do? Say no? Even if you knew better? Heck, no.

"Just a minute," I said. "I've got to get this on tape."*

---

*I always carry a pocket tape recorder with me. That probably sounds weird (by now you should know me), but it's perfect for saving all the special thoughts I don't want to lose. Then I type them into my computer diary at night. Whenever Dad sees me talking to my tape recorder, he says that I will make a great boss one day. Danny says I'm already bossy enough, thank you very much.

Roberto Wing's Ghost Story

Old Widow Hanson lived and died in this house. Only before she was Old Widow Hanson, she was Theodora Birchington. She lived on a farm near here. She didn't play with other children and always kept to herself. She talked to herself a lot, too. When she grew up, she got married to Hans Hanson who was a salesman.

Theodora and Hans fought a lot. The neighbors could hear them screaming at each other all night long. I don't know why she didn't just tell Hans to move out and then get a divorce, but they didn't have any kids so I guess she wasn't in any hurry. Then one time Hans tried to strangle her. That day she told everybody, "He's never going to do that again."

The next day, Hans disappeared. They found his body a few days later, only it was missing the hands. They had been cut off just above the wrist. His body is buried in the town cemetery. You can go see his grave, but his hands aren't there.

Anyway, people knew that Theodora had killed him, but they couldn't prove it, so she was never charged with murder.

Widow Hanson got older. She had wild wavy hair and a weird look in her eyes. And, like I said, she was really ugly. She was always talking to herself and screaming, "Get away! Get away!"

Then one day, when she was really old and ugly and after no one had seen her for weeks, the sheriff went looking for her. The neighbors had smelled something terrible, and I don't mean a skunk. The sheriff knocked the door down and searched the entire house, except the attic. Then he and his deputy opened the attic door. There was old Theodora, lying on her back at the bottom of the stairs with her neck broken.

The sheriff figured that she'd slipped at the top of the stairs and fallen to her death. Then they heard a strange sound. Drip drip drip. Coming from the top of the attic stairs. Drip drip drip.

They climbed the stairs and discovered a gruesome scene. There, lying on the floorboards, were the bloody hands of her husband. He had been dead for years, you know. The flesh was hanging off them and you could see the bones inside. The fingernails were all broken off and the fingertips were oozing blood. But the weird thing was the hands were covered with fresh blood—and it wasn't Widow Hanson's. The blood was dripping down the stairs. Drip drip drip. They followed the bloody trail to an old trunk where she must have kept the hands locked up. Inside it they found deep scratching gouges where the hands had clawed their way out.

The sheriff didn't know what of make of it, until he and the deputy turned Widow Hanson's body on her side. There on the back of her white nightgown were the prints of two bloody hands, prints that matched the hands of her husband. After all these years, the ghostly hands of Hans Hanson had come back from the dead to kill his widow.

People began to see her ghost in the house, but the scariest thing happened when the next family moved in. The husband was a truck driver. The first week they were there he was away, hauling a load of tomatoes. One night near the end of the week he called his wife to say he was coming home early and to wait up. But she fell asleep in what used to be Widow Hanson's bedroom. In the middle of the night she heard someone come into the room and she figured it was her husband. Then she heard someone get into bed with her. She was so sure it was her husband she didn't even open her eyes. She reached over and their hands met. He squeezed hers as if to say, "Goodnight." Then the woman fell back to sleep, holding her husband's hand.

In the morning the phone on the nightstand rang and woke her up. It was still dark, and the bedroom curtains were closed.

"Hello?" she said.

It was her husband. He was calling to say that his truck had broken down and not to worry, he'd be home soon. He hadn't wanted to call her in the middle of the night.

The woman's heart was pounding as she hung up the phone. Who had crawled into bed with her? And who had held her hand?

She jumped out of bed and turned on the light. The room was empty—or at least it looked that way. Then she forced her eyes to look at the bed. It seemed empty, too. So she caught her breath and decided that she had had the strangest dream. She climbed back into bed and pulled the covers up to her neck. She tried to go back to sleep, but she kept hearing a noise. A *dripping* noise. At first she wondered if there was a leak in the roof—only it hadn't been raining.

Drip drip drip.

The noise was getting louder. It seemed as

if it was coming from the other side of the bed. So she reached over and felt some liquid. Some *warm* liquid. She turned to look and pulled back the covers. There on the sheets next to her were the bloody handprints of Hans Hanson. And his blood was drip drip dripping on the floor.

The woman's husband found her—still alive, but she was never the same. They sold the house as soon as they could. That's why everybody calls it the Ghost House.

So two ghosts haunt your house now. Widow Hanson stands at the attic window and looks out . . . and just behind her are the creepy rotting hands of Hans waiting to push her down the stairs.

I was ready to hurl, but Danny looked like he believed every word Roberto had said, so I was going to put a stop to it.

"I don't believe in stupid ghosts like that," I said. "What do you do, write fake ghost stories or something?"

"I read all about it in the library," he said.

"The library?" Danny asked.

"Sometimes I go there and read old newspapers," he said. "I wouldn't let it scare me. I think you're lucky. I'd give anything to live in a haunted house."

"There's no such thing as a haunted house," I said. "It's just your imagination." I sounded exactly like Dad at his most logical.

"You're being very narrow-minded," Roberto said. "This isn't something that I'm making up. "You can read all about it in the San Luis Obispo paper."*

"No, thank you," I said. "This is a stupid, garbage ghost story. Ghosts and bloody fingerprints and all that stuff."

"How do you know?" he asked.

"Well, maybe I've seen a *real* ghost or two. And they weren't like that."

"I've seen some ghosts, too," he said. "This weird light floated into my room one night when I was four."

"What was it? The green slimer?" I asked.

Roberto ignored me. "And when I was in kindergarten I saw this shadowy ghost standing in the corner of our kitchen. And then Widow Hanson's ghost standing at the attic window. If I were you, I'd

*Don't even think about reading anything in the North Klondike newspaper; there isn't one. You'd have to read the Oro del Mar *Shore Times* (published weekly) for the boring local news. But if you want the really good stuff, Roberto says you have to get the S.L.O. papers.**

**You might as well learn that everyone around here uses S.L.O. instead of San Luis Obispo. I mean, why'd they even bother giving it a name?

look out. One article said that she likes to throw things."

I almost dropped the plate of cookies.

"What?"

Danny and I didn't even have to look at each other; we knew what we were both thinking.

"I said she likes to throw things. You know, to keep her husband's hands away."

"Your hairbrush . . . do you think. . . ?" Danny began to ask, before I could stop him.

"I don't think so," I said. "It just got knocked off my dresser. Anyway, remember what Dad says about ghosts."

"I know what I've seen in your attic window," Roberto said. "I've got an idea. Do you want to start a ghost club, twins?"

Roberto Wing had just made a MAJOR MISTAKE.

"Wait a minute!" I practically yelled, ready to jump all over him. "Don't *ever* use that word again!"

I scared him so much that I think he was ready to head home.

"What she means," Danny explained calmly, "is that we don't like that word."

"You mean *ghost*?" Roberto asked.

I sighed. "No, the T-word."

"Twins." Danny interpreted.

48

"You mean you're not *twins*?"

"Yes, we are, but that doesn't mean you get to call us that," I explained. "We don't like that word."

Now I'm only going to write this once for anyone reading my Ghost Book, so please pay attention: Danny and I were born one minute apart, which makes us a little unusual—but not *cute* (and definitely not *strange*). We don't like to use the T-word to explain who we are. Yes, we are twins, which is the last time you'll see that word written by me. Actually, I think of us as B.O.M.A.s: children who are Born One Minute Apart. Our mother did dress us alike when we were little, and then Dad took pictures to show how CUTE we looked, but Danny and I have hidden those pictures. Now we don't dress anything alike, but we're the same height and have the same color hair, even if Danny's is short and mine is long. We're just a brother and a sister. But some people are T-word-snoopers and can sniff us out by figuring out that we must be the same age.

"Oh, you look exactly alike," some blue-haired old T-word-snooper will say when she sees us with Dad at a mall.

"How do you tell them apart?" some dimwitted T-word-snooper with five snotty-nosed children will ask.

I could write a book about being a B.O.M.A., and

it wouldn't be one of those sweetie-pie T-word books either. Why do T-word-snoopers think T-words have to be identical? How could a Dante and a Christina have the same anatomy? Why do girls have to think that T-words are SO cute? Why does everyone think that T-words have to mean double-trouble? I've decided that there's a definite lack of brains when it comes to thinking about T-words. That's why I prefer B.O.M.A. (and you should, too!).*

"Okay, okay," Roberto said. "I'll never call you a T-word again, if you don't call me anything."

"Like what?"

"I don't know, but it would be a compound word . . . or," he smiled, "the name of a cereal."

"What do you mean?"

"Rice Chex. Howard Wheaton calls me Rice Chex."

"Who's he?"

"A humongous kid at school."

"Why does he call you that?"

"Because I'm half Chinese and half Mexican. He thinks he's really clever. *Ch* for Chinese, *ex* for Mexi-

---

*All right, I want to be fair and not leave anyone out. You can be a T-word and not be a B.O.M.A., depending on how far apart you were born. So there are definitely B.T.M.A.s and B.F.M.A.s, except it gets confusing. Does T stand for two or three minutes? Does F stand for four or five minutes? And what about B.S.T.D.A.s? Some T-words in the *National Enquirer* are Born Sixty-Two Days Apart. I mean, when you get right down to it, what difference does it make when anyone is born?

can. Put them all together and they spell cereal. He must think I eat a lot of rice or something. He's not very enlightened. So I call him Shredded Wheat."

"Why?"

"Because he has a dumb, soggy brain."

"Okay," I said. "I promise."

"Promise," Danny agreed.

"So do you want to have a ghost club?"

"Sure," Danny said.

"What about you, Christina?" Roberto asked.

"She's in," Danny answered.

"I didn't say that," I replied.

"I can tell you want to," Danny said.

"I do not," I said.

"You do, too."

"Oh, fine," I agreed. "I'll be in your dumb ghost club. But there aren't any ghosts to find. So it's really a waste of time."

I could always quit, I told myself, if it was silly.

"I have a name for it," Roberto said. "Ghost Hunters I.N.K. That stands for In North Klondike."

"I like it," Danny said.

"How long have you been waiting to do this?" I asked. "Your whole life?"

"No," said Roberto. "Just recently."

And that's how our club got started. Roberto was

totally to blame (it was HIS idea), but so was my brain.

What if Widow Hanson and her husband, Hans, and his hands are still around? I was thinking. *And what if they don't want us living in their weird house?*

5

Ghosts in the Attic

"Let's have a stakeout," Roberto proposed next.

My heart began pounding.

"There aren't any ghosts," I said.

"You saw what happened to your hairbrush," Danny said.

"Let's check it out," Roberto urged. "Maybe we could spend the night in the attic."

Spend the night in the attic? Roberto was taking this a little too seriously. "Let's talk to Dad about this," I suggested.

"There's nothing in our attic," Dad said after I had told him about Widow Hanson. He couldn't have sounded more definite. "And there's certainly no ghost in this house."

"See?" I told them.

"Really, Mr. Rose, Widow Hanson's ghost lives here," Roberto said. "It says so in the newspaper."

"Roberto, newspapers say a lot of things but that doesn't make them true," Dad said. "I have not seen Widow Hanson anywhere, or this husband of hers—"

"Or his hands," I added.

"—and I have cleaned this place from top to bottom, haven't I, Christina?"

I nodded. Dad wasn't exactly Mr. Clean, so I doubted that he had checked the dust and cobwebs in every corner.

"Maybe she was hiding," Roberto said. "Maybe she only comes out at night, when you're not cleaning. That's when I saw her. Maybe the hands are waiting for just the right time to attack."

"And maybe she only appears to certain children," Dad said, "with very active and creative imaginations. The Mazzas didn't have any ghosts floating around—and they lived here for ten years."

Dad was missing the point. The Mazzas' taste in decorating was enough to scare any ghost back to the grave.

Then Danny added his two cents: "If we spent the night in the attic, we'd find out for sure."

"You wouldn't want us to do that, would you, Dad?" I asked. "It's not very comfortable."

"Christina, I don't believe in ghosts, but I don't

think it would be so bad to explore this and get it out of your system. So if that's what you want. . . ."

"But, Dad—"

"Come to think of it," he said, "maybe this is your lucky day. I just found out today who our other neighbor is. It's Professor Barrymore. I haven't seen him yet, but there was a little article in the *Shore Times* today. Here, let me show you."

In a moment, he produced the tiniest of articles:

N. KLONDIKE PROFESSOR PUBLISHES NEW BOOK

Parapsychologist and professor I. Barrymore of Mid-Coastal California College has published a book entitled, *Investigations of Supernatural Phenomena*. Professor Barrymore's previous book was *A Practical Guide to Ghost Hunting*.

"Maybe you should talk to Professor Barrymore," he suggested.

"I thought you said there aren't any ghosts," I said.

"Well, a lot of people think they're real. Maybe you've found a real adventure here."

A real adventure! Dad's idea of adventure was making a casserole with tuna packed in oil instead of water. He wasn't going to go up in the attic with us— not that *I* wanted him to. I knew what he was thinking. He was trying to help Danny take his mind off Sparky. He thought a ghost adventure was just the thing.

"You kids have fun," he said, heading for the kitchen door. "I'm running out for some groceries. Be back soon."

"Come on," Roberto insisted, "let's go to the attic."

I could have gone back outside to play soccer by myself and let the boys explore the attic for ghosts, but a tiny voice in my brain was talking to me: *What's in the attic, Christina? What if it's a ghost? Or two? What if Widow Hanson or her husband is haunting you?*

"Okay," I agreed.

"Wait a second," Roberto said. "I have to go home and get my equipment."

"What equipment?" I was picturing a bulldozer and a wrecking ball.

"My ghost hunting equipment," he said, and took off.

He was back in two minutes, carrying a small backpack.

"What's in there?" Danny asked.

"You'll see," Roberto said. He strapped it on his back and we were ready to go.

We had six bedrooms on the second floor and a stairway behind a closed door that led to the attic.*

---

*You probably wondered why Dad bought a house with six bedrooms. Like, he's planning on getting remarried and having more kids—NOT! He said the house was being foreclosed and it was a steal. I told him stealing wasn't nice and he should return it immediately. He said no one would want it. He's absolutely right, you know.

"It's kind of dark up there," Danny said, pointing to the attic door. "There's only one light bulb."

"Don't be such a dimwit," Roberto joked. "This will be an illuminating experience."

He put his hand on the doorknob.

"If you're so brave," I said, "you go ahead. You can be first."

Roberto talked a good game, but when it came time to open the attic door, he seemed a little nervous. He looked like he was expecting to see Widow Hanson's bloody body behind the door, grinning toothlessly at us. But nothing was there except the dark wood stairs and a couple of empty boxes.

Then Danny said, "Here's the light," and Roberto jumped a mile.

"What's wrong?" Danny asked.

"Nothing," Roberto said. He walked two creaky steps up and stopped. He listened, then took two more steps. Each time he stepped up, a slow creak sounded. "Come on. There's nothing here."

Danny went next, and I began to follow him. By the time we reached the top of the stairway, everything was quiet. The light bulb hung down right over the stairs, and the attic sprawled in every dark and shadowy direction. There used to be four stained glass windows (one on each wall of the attic), only now they were boarded up. It was so dark in the farthest parts that it looked like moonless nights where the darkness goes on forever.

"This is where the hands pushed her," Roberto whispered.

"Where's the trunk?" Danny asked.

"There's no trunk like that up here," I said. "It's all our stuff."

"No, it's not," Danny said. "This isn't ours."

He pointed at a large wooden wardrobe standing to the side of the stairs.

"Well, there's no trunk," I said.

"Shh!" Roberto warned. Then he removed his backpack. He unzipped a small front pocket and reached in.

"What are you doing?" I whispered.

"Watch," he said.

First, he pulled out a plastic bag full of flour and began to sprinkle it on the floorboards near the stairs.

"Why are you doing that?" I asked.

"To see if the ghost leaves footprints," he said. "If it does, then it's just a robber."

Then he removed a large thermometer and read the temperature.

"Seventy-nine degrees," he said.

"What's that for?" Danny asked.

"If there's a ghost, it's going to get cold in here. We can tell by reading the thermometer."

Next he pulled out a small notebook attached to a

wristband. He slipped the wristband onto his left wrist. The notebook and a small pen attached with string dangled from his arm.

"I'm right-handed," he explained.

"That's nice," I said. "What do you need it for?"

"In case I need to write some notes."

"Where did you get all these ideas from?" I asked. He was definitely crazier than me.

"From a book. It tells you all about ghosts and how to hunt for them. I know it sounds strange but it's true."

"Who wrote it?"

"I forget—except I think the author's name rhymes with scream."

Finally, I watched him pull a handful of pebbles from the backpack.

He took one and tossed it into a corner. It made a tapping sound as it landed, then everything was quiet. He aimed a pebble at another dark corner. Another tap, then nothing. I guess Roberto thought that the ghost would come running if it got hit by a pebble.

By the time he tried every dark spot, he had gotten a little braver. In a moment of complete bravery (not to mention stupidity) Roberto threw the rest of the pebbles against the darkest wall. Tap tap, thud, tap, thud thud, tap. We heard them all hit.

Then the rustling began. Rustle, rustle. Like rattlesnakes in paper bags, like lions wrapped in starchy parachutes, like . . . GHOSTS IN OUR ATTIC!

Or like a suitcase sliding onto some wadded-up packing paper. That's what it was.

"It's just a suitcase," I said, walking over to it. "Look, it just slid off the pile here."

"Are you sure?" Roberto asked.

That was when I saw an old chew-toy that belonged to Sparky. We must have packed it by accident. I picked it up and inspected it.

"What's that?" Danny asked.

"One of Sparky's rawhides," I said.

"Who's Sparky?" Roberto said.

"Our dog," I said.

"*My* dog," Danny corrected.

"He was too old, he had to stay in New York," I explained.

"Oh, you're better off," Roberto said. "I think dogs are a lot of trouble."

Just then, an old wardrobe standing behind Roberto began to move. It rocked back and forth, its feet scraping on the attic floorboards.

"Jump!" I yelled to Roberto. I grabbed him and pulled him away.

Roberto dropped his thermometer and we ran downstairs so fast I don't even remember it. But I do remember locking the attic door. I thought about swallowing the key. I had become a definite believer in the attic ghosts—whoever or whatever they were.

That's when we went to my room and I wrote a letter to Professor Barrymore on my computer:

PROFESSOR BARRYMORE:

THIS IS URGENT! YOU MUST HELP US. WE ARE HAVING TROUBLE WITH GHOSTS! WE STARTED A GHOST HUNTERS CLUB BUT WE DON'T KNOW WHAT TO DO WITH THE GHOST IN OUR ATTIC. DANNY AND I LIVE NEXT DOOR TO YOU (AND ROBERTO LIVES ACROSS THE STREET). WE KNOW YOU STUDY GHOSTS AND HAVE WRITTEN BOOKS ABOUT THEM SO COULD YOU STOP BY AND SEE WHAT YOU CAN DO? PLEASE? WE ARE DESPERATE! THE GHOST TRIED TO KILL ROBERTO TODAY!

YOUR NEIGHBOR,
CHRISTINA ROSE

6

A Tricky Ghost

Danny and I didn't know Professor Barrymore. Even Roberto had never seen him. He must not have made much money at the university because he wasn't good at keeping up his house. Or maybe the hippies that had owned our house had lived in his house, too. The only nice thing about Professor Barrymore's house was a new garage attached to the side.

"Maybe he's like Bruce Wayne," Roberto said as we stood on the sidewalk. "I bet he parks his Ghostmobile there. Do you think the tires have spooks—I mean, spokes?"

"Very funny," I said. "I don't think Bruce Wayne would live in a house like this."

"You're right," Roberto said. "But it does look like it could *cave* in. It doesn't look like he's home. Do you think he's out *Robin* something?"

"Yuck, yuck," I said. "You're such a Joker."

"Go ahead," Danny said, nudging me. "Deliver the letter."

"Yeah, come on," Roberto said.

"Why should I take it over?" I asked. "You do it. The club was your idea."

"But you're the president," Roberto said.

"The president?"

"Yes," Roberto explained, "Christina Rose, President of Ghost Hunters I.N.K."

"Maybe, but—"

"And you were the best writing the letter to Professor Barrymore," Danny said. "Presidents have to be good writers. Right?"

"Yes, but—"

"And the president gets to run the meetings."

"All right," I said, warming up to the idea, "but you have to do what I say if I'm president."

"Sure," Roberto agreed.

"Just a minute," Danny complained, "I don't want her to boss me around."

"Make her happy," Roberto said, "or you'll be the president."

I started up the front walk.

Why am I doing this? I asked myself. *Two big sixth-grade boys, and I'm the one who has to deliver a ghost letter?*

I stepped lightly onto the porch and placed the letter inside the mailbox. Then I took off.

By now Roberto and Danny were conveniently waiting in our front yard.

"Did you give it to him?" Roberto asked.

"I put it in his mailbox," I said. I watched as Dad pulled the car into the driveway. "I wasn't going to ring the doorbell and bother him. He might be busy."

"I told you not to put it in the mailbox," Roberto said. "That's a federal offense. You didn't mail it. And anyway, he might not get it till tomorrow. We need help tonight!"

"Can *I* get some help?" Dad asked, stepping onto the porch carrying two bags of groceries. "And what are you all up to?"

"Nothing," Danny said. And I wasn't going to say anything different.

After we helped carry the groceries into the house, Dad said, "Roberto, why don't you ask your mom if the two of you can come for dinner tonight? Then you can spend the night in the attic."

"Well, maybe tonight isn't so good for staying in the attic," Roberto said. "Maybe another night. But I'll go ask about dinner."

"Good idea," Danny agreed.

None of us was going to step into that attic again—not without a real ghost hunter around.

Mme. Olga was just pouring herself a glass of iced tea when we walked into the kitchen. She didn't look anything like the Mme. Olga I pictured. She had shaggy brown hair, unpainted nails, and no makeup (she didn't need it at all). She was wearing blue jeans, a pink T-shirt, and little silver half-moon earrings. Very normal, I thought, especially for North Klondike. Except her perfume smelled like incense.

"Hi, kids," she said. "You must be Christina and Danny."

"That's right," I said. "Are you really Madame Olga."

"Oh, don't call me that. Olga's my middle name. I just use it for my psychic work. Most people call me by my first name: Carol. You can call me that." Then she scanned our faces and said, "Were you kids just doing a little ghost hunting?"

"How did you know?" I asked.

"Be careful what you're thinking," Roberto warned.

"Stop scaring them," Carol said quickly. "I know you very well, Roberto. I know that you've got ghosts on the brain. And you told me you've been reading all about Widow Hanson—"

"—and making up stuff about her," I added.

"Oh, is he telling his Widow Hanson ghost story again?" Carol asked. "I think it gets more gruesome every time."

"I know," I said, "I told him ghosts aren't like that."

"That may be, but you have to watch out for ghosts all the same," Carol said. "You never know what you might find."

"What do you mean?" I asked.

"My father told me a ghost story not long before he died. It gives me the chills to think about it."

"Not that one," Roberto whined.

"Now, Roberto," Carol said. "Sit down, kids, this ghost will give you something to think about."

Mme. Olga's Ghost Story

Papi, my grandfather, God rest his soul, worked very hard. He came from Mexico without much money. With a little luck and a lot of hard work he managed to buy a small truck farm outside Sacramento. Later, he saved more money and bought another one, about forty miles away.

Papi had to travel between the farms a lot,

you know, to make sure they were running smoothly. It wasn't that he didn't trust anyone, but he had to stay on top of things. He didn't speak much English but he knew how to run a farm.

One day he is driving to one of the farms in his new Buick convertible. It is *un diá esplendido*. A beautiful day. All of a sudden, Papi has to pee. You know, he was a wonderful man, but he had the smallest bladder. He used to joke that liquid went through him so fast that he should drink and pee at the same time.

Anyway, he stops on the side of the road near some bushes. After he's done, he hears a child's voice. At first it's so faint he doesn't pay attention. He figures it's just a kid playing. Then the voice gets louder and he realizes that the child needs help. He runs and finds a little girl—a little blond girl—lying half in the water. She looks like such a little angel, but she's in bad shape. It looks like she was almost drowned.

The sides of the ditch are steep, but Papi uses a tree branch to help pull the girl to him. Somehow he picks her up and carries her to his car and props her up in the back seat. It's warm but she's shivering, so he takes a blanket from the trunk and puts it around her to dry her off. Then he decides to take her home.

"Where do you live?" he asks her. "Where are your parents?" Only he's talking in Spanish. *"¿Dónde vive Ud.? ¿Dónde están sus padres?"*

She looks at him like he's crazy, you know, so he figures she doesn't speak Spanish. And his English was no good. So he points down the road and the girl nods.

Anyway, to make a long ghost story short, he starts driving and motioning. This way? That way? He points and she keeps nodding or shaking her head. In a little while she points at the driveway of this big fancy farm of some hotshot Anglos. "Here," the girl says. Then she scoots down on the seat and falls asleep.

The farm is so big that the house is two miles off the main road, so Papi never even knew it was there before. He drives up to the house and starts to run to the front door. A man and woman come rushing out to him.

"What do you want?" they ask, sounding worried.

"Little girl," he says.

"You found her? Where is she?"

"En el coche. En el asiento de atrás," he says. "In the back seat."

The couple run to the car but they don't see any little girl there. Only a wadded up blanket in the back seat.

"Where is she?" they ask.

"Here. *Aquí. Ella estaba aquí en el coche*," he tells them in Spanish. "She was here in the car," he says.

Then he picks up the blanket, but it is bone dry.

He tries to tell them that he found her but now she's gone. But his English doesn't help, and their Spanish is worse. So he decides to show them the irrigation ditch where he found the girl.

He drives them back to the place where he had stopped to pee. The couple jump out and there, lying face down in the water, is the body of the little blond girl. *La niña rubia. Muerta.* She's dead.

Do you know what happened? To my poor, foolish Papi? He didn't carry that poor little girl to the car. He carried her *ghost!*

Danny's mouth was hanging open again.

"Is that true?" he asked.

"Of course it's true," Carol said. "But that's not the end of it. You want to know what happened next? This is the most terrible part of all."

"Say no," Roberto warned.

"Too late," Carol told us.

So the man and the woman call the police and tell them that Papi killed their little girl. He's Mexican, after all. So they have him arrested and charged with her murder. He doesn't understand. He had nothing to do with that little girl, only her ghost. How do you tell that to the police?

Then he needs money for a lawyer, so he has to sell one of his farms. Everything drags on, so he has to sell the other farm. He loses money because he can't even wait for a good offer.

Then, wouldn't you know? Right before the trial starts, the little girl's brother speaks up. He was playing with his sister and he pushed her into the water. It was steep and she couldn't climb out and he couldn't help her and she drowned.

And do you know those people never even said they were sorry to my grandfather? That ghost ruined him. He lost everything. Two months later, he was dead. Forty-nine, my grandfather was. Much too young. And all because of a ghost.

"That's my story, *muchachos y muchacha*. So just be careful what you go looking for in that attic of yours. You don't want to find a tricky ghost. You may get more than you bargained for."

"We already did," I said. "Actually, we came over to ask you a question."

"I know," Carol said. "Roberto and I would love to come to dinner. It was nice of your father to ask. I've got a caramel chocolate chip apple crisp in the freezer. I'll bring it over and bake it in your oven for dessert."

She was positively scary—and very, very nice.

Over a dinner of Dad's special tuna gazpacho soup, we told Dad and Carol what had happened in the attic.

"So now there are all these pebbles all over my attic floor?" he asked. We nodded. "You're sure you didn't break anything? Your mother's good china is up there."

"We were being careful," I said.

"I love the soup," Carol said, after her first spoonful. "Do you have any salt?"

Dad looked at her like she had cursed.

"Salt?"

"Yes, just a little," Carol said. "I like a little salt in my soup."

"Do you know what salt can do to you? "

"Well, maybe to you, but not to me. I just wanted a little salt."

"I'm sorry," Dad said. "We don't have any salt in the—"

Suddenly Carol held up her hand to stop him. "Just a minute," she said. "A woman's going to ring the doorbell."

At that very moment, the doorbell rang.

Dad looked at Carol suspiciously, then went to answer the door.

"How did you know that?" Danny asked.

Carol smiled.

"I was hoping it would be Professor Barrymore," I said.

At that moment, Dad came back into the kitchen.

"Christina, there's a woman to see you."

"Me?" I asked. "Who knows me in North Klondike?"

I walked through the living room to the front door.

Standing on the porch was a tall thin woman with a very pale face. She was dressed in black: pants, turtleneck, hat—and cape. She looked ten feet tall.

"You must be Christina," she said, peering down at me. When she opened her mouth, I swear I saw fangs.

"Yes."

"Well, let me introduce myself," she said,

extending a hand with two-inch-long blood-red fingernails. "I am Imogen Barrymore, your next-door neighbor. But let's dispense with the pleasantries, shall we, so as not to waste any more time? I received your note. Please, take me to see your ghost."

7

Onward and Upward

"Dad," I called, "it's Professor Barrymore! She wants to see our ghost."

Everyone came running to the front hall.

"Hello, Mrs. Rose?" Professor Barrymore said. Danny and I quickly looked at Carol, Roberto looked at Dad.

Dad said, "This is Mrs. Wing. She lives across the street."

"How nice to meet you," she said, shaking hands. "I understand there's a ghost in the attic."

"Actually, there's two," I said.

"Maybe three," Roberto added.

"Three? No way."

"It depends on if the hands work together or separately," he explained.

"The number is unimportant. However, I would love to go upstairs and have a look around,"

Professor Barrymore said. "Would that be all right?"

"Certainly," Dad said.

"But aren't you going to be late for your party?" Carol asked.

She cocked her head and looked closely at Carol.

"Yes, a bit. We're having a little soiree tonight—a costume party, actually. But tell me, exactly how long have you had your psychic ability?"

"Since I was six, I guess," Carol replied, then stopped to sniff the air. "Oh, my God, the apple crisp, it's burning!"

The faint smell of burned sugar drifted past my nose as Carol and Dad rushed into the kitchen.

"Do you want us to tell you about the ghost?" Roberto asked.

Professor Barrymore checked her watch, rolled her eyes around once, and pondered the question.

Then she told Roberto, "I think not. The very first rule of investigating paranormal phenomena is this: Do not say you've seen a ghost unless you know what you've actually seen. You have had an unusual and perhaps frightening experience. The question is not, *How did a ghost get into my attic?* The question is, *Did this so-called paranormal experience involve a ghost?* I wouldn't presume to say so at this point, if I were you."

Roberto looked very disappointed.

"And the second rule is," Professor Barrymore continued, producing a floral bag from under her cape, "don't talk about what you've seen with anyone. You must write a report that contains all the facts and pertinent details." She extracted a pile of papers. The top one said "Ghost Report Form." "I'm going to give each of you a few report forms to record information about your experience. But no talking about your stories. You might contaminate them."

"What do you mean, contaminate?" Roberto asked.

"Quite simply, when you tell Christina what you saw, she may begin to believe that she saw the same thing. Actually, she may have seen something quite different, but the stories begin to blend together and they become contaminated. Until you've each had a chance to write a report, stop chatting with each other about the experience. It may already be too late."

"Should we write it now?" I asked.

"No time for that, duckie," she said. "I simply need to have a quick look-see at the attic. Don't tell me anything about what happened. Who's going to lead the way?"

"The president of our club is the leader," Roberto said.

"Great," I said. I should have known it would come back to haunt me. "Follow me."

"Onward," Professor Barrymore urged as we climbed the attic stairs. We must have looked really weird. Danny, Roberto, me, making our way up the attic stairs like a team of reluctant huskies, and Professor Barrymore bringing up the rear in her cape and fangs. "Onward," she repeated. "Never fear a paranormal experience."

At the top of the stairs we stood facing the wardrobe. We weren't going to let it get the jump on us again. Despite the dim light, Professor Barrymore headed straight for the darkest area of the attic.

"What am I walking in?" she asked. "Rat poison?"

"Flour," Roberto said proudly. "Actually, it's ghost-catching powder."

"I see," she said.

She pushed past empty boxes and marched to the back wall to one of the boarded windows. She bent down and looked at the floor under the window. Then she stood up and faced us.

"Hmmm," she said.

"What?" Roberto asked.

She put her index finger to her lips and tapped it three times. "Interesting."

"What's interesting?" Danny asked.

She waved her hand in the air. "Mum's the word," she warned.

Then Professor Barrymore began to walk along the perimeter of the attic. Every now and then, especially when she came to each of the three remaining windows, she stopped and squatted down to inspect the floor. By the time she finished checking the outside wall, she walked back to the stairs.

"Let's go, shall we?" she said, and tramped down the stairs.

"But what did you find?" I asked as we followed her.

"I found enough flour to bake a chocolate gateau, that's for certain," she said, trying to dust off her boots.

"But is there a ghost?" Roberto asked.

"I cannot discuss this now," she said when we had all reached the second-floor hallway. "I've just begun my investigation. These things take time, you know."

"But can't you tell us what you think you saw up there?" I asked.

"Birds," she said.

"Birds?" Danny asked.

"Birds. There is evidence of birds having inhabited the attic."

"But we didn't see any birds," Roberto said. "We saw—"

"Do *not*," she said quite sharply, "tell me what you saw. I saw evidence of birds. That does not mean anything at this point. I am simply saying that birds have been in your attic. I am not speaking about ghosts or anything of that nature. And if you want me to carry this investigation any further, you will each have to write a report tonight about what you saw and experienced. Please bring them to my house tomorrow. And please, won't you all be so kind as to use your best penmanship and write in ink? My eyesight is not what it used to be."

She checked her watch again.

"I really must go," she said. "T.T.F.N."

"What?" Roberto said.

"Ah, a puzzlement!" she said. "T.T.F.N. means Ta-Ta For Now. T.T.F.N., children! I have a werewolf to meet. See me to the door, Christina. You boys can start your reports. I believe you have a lot to tell me."

With that, she marched down to the front hall. I trailed behind her; Danny and Roberto headed for the kitchen.

At the front door she said, "This has been most interesting. I never know when a new case will pop up. I certainly never expected it next door."

"You haven't heard about Widow Hanson or her husband?" I asked.

"Who is that, dear?"

"An old woman who used to live in our house. A

woman who killed her husband and then his ghost killed her." I gave her all the details. "At least that's what Roberto says. But I don't believe him at all."

"Widow Hanson? Haven't heard of her, but such a story shouldn't be too hard to check. I must admit, however, that it sounds like a young boy's tall tale to my well-trained ears."

"That's what I thought, too. I told him that ghosts weren't like that."

"Exactly," Professor Barrymore said. Then she raised her eyebrows and peered at me a little more closely. "But how would you know that, dear? Have you had any other paranormal experiences?"

"Oh, uh, well, I—"

"It's nothing to be ashamed of, you know. Certainly not. I would never hesitate to say that something unusual—even quite bizarre—occurred, if it had. Except, of course, to certain rude and unsavory characters who consider the investigation of the paranormal to be claptrap. But I, Imogen Barrymore, am not one of those people. Hardly, my dear. Let me tell you something; my werewolf will have to wait. I not only investigate all sorts of paranormalities, I have experienced a few myself, firsthand. So let me fill you in on my very first experience. Do you have a moment or two?"

Of course I did. Who wouldn't, if there was a ghost story to be told?

Professor Barrymore's First Ghost Story

I grew up in the Yorkshire Dales. Have you heard of it, dear? That's an area in the north of England. Perhaps you have read *Wuthering Heights*? Seen the movie, perhaps? Good—you looked like the type of girl who would. That's where I grew up, near the town of Harrogate.

I lived with my father and my mother and later my grandfather, who came to stay with us when he fell ill. One day when I was twelve I came home from school, closed the front door, walked down the hallway to the kitchen, said hello to my grandfather, who was sitting at the kitchen table having a cup of tea as he always did, and then went upstairs to my room to begin my schoolwork.

It was then—and only then, my dear—that I remembered my grandfather had been dead for one month. I shivered a moment—quite a natural reaction. But I loved my grandfather more than anything, and I raced down the stairway to the kitchen, hoping that he would still be there. He was not. I cried for a time, and then reason overtook me. I made a decision to determine exactly what had happened.

Had I seen his ghost? I was certain that I had. I sat down in my room and wrote everything that I remembered. What I saw as I had walked into the kitchen, what I heard, what I smelled, what I sensed. It was not an easy thing to do. I was certain that I had seen him, but I could not say with certainty if he looked at me, if he moved, if the kettle was still steaming, if his teacup sat on the table. Still, I was able to write ten pages of details describing what had happened. This was my very first ghost report.

Of course, my parents thought I had lost my mind completely. And, of course, my grandfather never reappeared. But I was well on my way to becoming an investigator, and I have no apologies to make, and nothing to be ashamed or embarrassed about.

"And neither do you, my dear," she said, tapping my nose with one of her Dracula nails. "But I must run. Will you think about what I've said? Will you think about telling me what else has happened?"

I was going to tell her I would, but she said "T.T.F.N." again and took off like a bat before sunrise before I could say another word.

8

The Phantom Apple Crisp

In no time, we were all back at the table, and Carol was serving her salvaged apple crisp.

"Sorry about the oven," Dad was saying. "I think it's running hotter than it should. I'll have to call a service person tomorrow."

"That's okay," Carol said. "It wasn't totally ruined. Would you like some? There's plenty."

"Well, maybe just the apple part," Dad said. "None of the crisp . . . or that." He pointed to a bowl of whipped cream. We all watched as Roberto put a gloppy spoonful of it on his apple crisp.

"We're only allowed to have skim milk," I explained. "I don't think you can make whipped cream out of that."

"What about ice cream?" Carol asked. "I couldn't live without ice cream."

"Fat-free frozen yogurt," Danny told her.

"Ugh," Carol said. "That's like mixing cardboard and water and freezing it and calling it food."

"I see we have very different beliefs when it comes to food," Dad said.

"I think we have very different *taste* in food," Carol corrected.

"Well, the apples are good," Dad said.

"They should be," Carol said. "They have lots of cinnamon and nutmeg and ginger mixed with them and butter to make them—"

Dad dropped his fork. "Butter?" he asked. You would have thought he had just eaten a dead squirrel. "With the apples?"

"Yes, with the apples," Carol said.

"You should have told me."

"You didn't tell me you wanted me to tell you."

Danny, Roberto, and I were looking at each other, almost smiling. You would have thought they were married, the way they were arguing.

"Why don't we change the subject?" Dad suggested.

"Yes," Carol agreed, "I was just about to say that I'm so glad Roberto and Christina and Danny have become such good friends. Roberto's needed a few friends lately and—"

"Mom!" Roberto protested.

"Okay, okay," she said, backing off. "It's just that his father's sick, and now that we're divorced, Roberto doesn't get to see him very often."

"Okay, Mom," Roberto said. "End of discussion."

I wanted to ask what was wrong with Roberto's dad, but I didn't dare.

"Can you tell us what's going to happen with the ghost in the attic?" Danny asked Carol. "I mean, using your Powers and stuff."

"No, and I can't tell you what clothes you're going to wear tomorrow or the next time the phone's going to ring either."

"Or if the apple crisp is going to burn," I added.

"Christina, you are one smart girl," Carol said.

"Then how did you know that Professor Barrymore was going to ring the doorbell?" Danny asked.

"Think about what you just said. Did I say that Professor Barrymore was going to ring the bell? Or did I say something else?"

"You said . . . let's see," Danny began. "You said a woman was going to ring the bell."

"Right."

"So how did you know that?"

Carol threw her hands into the air and said in an exasperated tone, "Because I looked through that window and saw a woman stepping onto the porch!"

"But I thought you were psychic," Danny said, very confused.

"Let me tell you about my Powers," Carol said. "If you lose something, like car keys, I can probably help you find them. If you're in the room with me, sometimes I can tell what you're thinking. And if something strange is happening, I can usually pick up on it in a hurry. But I can't tell the future, and I can't help you win the lottery, so don't ask me for six numbers. If I could do that, I wouldn't be sitting here right now—well, that's not true—I'd just be sitting here with a lot more money in my bank account."

"So what can you tell us?" Danny asked. "Anything?"

"Let's do this," Carol said. "I'll try to do a little reading for everyone, except Roberto, who gets a reading any time he wants and especially when he doesn't. But I need to have only one person at the table with me. John, you can be first," she told my dad. "The rest of you can stand over there by the refrigerator."

We got up and left Dad and Carol at the table.

"Why don't you start with Danny or Christina?" Dad suggested. "It'll be more fun for them."

"What Dad means is that you can't tell him anything anyway," I joked.

"You never know what I'll uncover. Now be quiet."

"Whatever you say."

"Okay," Carol said, closing her eyes and sitting very still. "Nobody talk, and let me see what I see. I see a tunnel, a long tunnel—no, it's not a tunnel, it's a blood vessel. I see it getting clogged up with globs of gooey butter. Oh, no, I see where I am. I'm in your dad's arteries after he ate the apple crisp! Help! Get me out of here!"

"Very funny," Dad said.

"No, really," Danny said. "What do you see?"

"Okay," she said. "I'll get serious. Sometimes I just get feelings about people. But at this time I'm getting a strong image. It seems to come from a woman with long brown hair. It seems to come from a J. Could her name start with J? I can't tell. It seems to come from a woman wearing a light coat and a necklace. It seems to come from holding a heart necklace, and she's—"

"Okay," Dad interrupted. "I think that's enough."

I was totally shocked. "That was Mom," I said.

"Mom," Danny repeated.

"I don't want to hear any more," Dad said.

"There's nothing else to say," Carol told him. "Except it seems to come from words. Words on the heart. Does that make any sense?"

"What'd you do? See the picture on my dresser?" Dad asked. He had framed the last picture he had ever taken of Mom—the same one in my Remember Me locket—and put it on his dresser. Carol had described it perfectly.

"I haven't been upstairs," Carol said.

"Okay, all right. Then you saw Christina's locket."

"This?" I asked, pulling it out from under my top. "Hardly. I don't wear it out. I don't want to damage it."

"Then, how—?"

"Calm down, Dad," I said. He was definitely spooked—and so was I, a little. So I asked Carol, "Do you mean that our mom is here in this room with us right now?"

"Not really," Carol said. "It isn't as if her ghost is here, hiding behind the door." We all turned and looked at the kitchen door then, fully expecting her ghost to materialize. "I just get strong feelings sometimes about people or things. Maybe her spirit is here. Maybe it's a mental image of your mother that your father keeps in his head. I don't really know."

"Do Danny next," I said.

Danny didn't want to hang around for a reading, but Dad put his hands on Danny's shoulders and guided him into a chair. "Sit here," Dad said. "I'm going to do the dishes."

"Why didn't you hook up the dishwasher?" Roberto asked. The new dishwasher was sitting right in the middle of the kitchen floor.

"Because I don't know how," Dad said. "I'll have to call a plumber tomorrow."

"I can help you," Carol said. "I can hook up or repair almost anything—especially if it saves money."

"Do Danny's reading," I urged.

"Just a minute," Carol said. When she was ready, she said, "It's kind of funny, but I get an image of a dog. Is that weird, or what? It seems to come from a little dog."

"What kind is it?" Danny asked.

"I don't know anything about dogs, really," Carol said. "But it seems to come from white, whiteness."

"Did you tell her, Dad?" I asked.

"I haven't said anything about it," Dad said.

"It's Sparky," Danny told Carol. "You saw Sparky."

"And I see a red ball," Carol added. "Right in the dog's mouth."

"How did you know?" Danny asked.

"If I knew," Carol said, "I'd be a millionaire."

"But what about Sparky?" Danny asked.

"Nothing," Carol said. "I just feel his presence in this room."

"But he's in New York," Danny said.

"All I can say is that there are a lot of brainwaves about Sparky right here. I bet you really miss him."

"Yeah—" I started to say. But just then the dish of apple crisp slid off the stove and crashed onto the floor by Dad's feet. It shattered to pieces and sprayed bits of apple crisp and glass on the bottom of his jeans.

"Are you okay?" Carol asked.

"I think so," Dad said. "I'm glad I wasn't wearing shorts or my legs would have been cut to shreds."

Carol stepped carefully over to Dad.

"There's glass everywhere," she said. "I'll get the broom."

"It's in the—"

"I know where it is," Carol said and retrieved it from the back of the basement door. In a short time they had cleaned up everything. The only thing left of the apple crisp was the burned smell in the kitchen.

"I know you didn't like it," Carol said finally, "but you didn't have to throw it on the floor."

"I didn't touch it," Dad said. "I was doing the dishes."

"It didn't slip out of your hands?"

"No, I was washing the plates."

"Then how did it get on the floor?"

Roberto, Danny, and I looked at each other.

"Widow Hanson," we said.

"Or her husband, Hans," I added.

"Or her husband's hands," Roberto joked.

"Come on, kids," Dad said. "The dish just slipped."

"It's Widow Hanson," Roberto said. "I told you. Where's Professor Barrymore when you need her?"

"Just a minute," Carol said. "The dish was—"

"Remember what Professor Barrymore said?" I interrupted. "We should write the ghost reports before we talk about anything. I'll go get some report forms and we can write down what we saw before we talk about it."

"What time is it?" Roberto was asking when I walked back in the room.

"Six forty-two," Dad said. "Why?"

"We should probably know what time it happened. That might be important. It happened some time between six thirty-five and six-forty."

"Start writing," I said. "No talking."

Within ten minutes everyone was finished writing their accounts. Danny's was the most artistic. He hates to write, so he drew his report.

Dad's was the shortest:

> *I was washing dishes, and a dish of apple crisp that had been sitting safely on the stove fell onto the floor. I hadn't touched it, and I only saw it after it crashed. It made a huge mess. Carol cleaned it up (thank you). If it was done by a ghost, it was definitely a ghost that hated fat-laden high-cholesterol overly sweet food!*

Everyone else took the matter seriously, though we saw different things. Carol didn't see anything because her back was to the stove. But she knew where the dish had been sitting. Danny and I saw the shattered dish after it hit the floor. And Roberto, who had been facing the stove, said he actually saw the dish moving across the burners before it fell off onto the floor.

"Are you telling the truth?" I asked.

"I know what I saw," he said.

"You didn't SEE Widow Hanson's ghost," I said.

"It had to be her," Roberto said. "Or the hands of Hans."

"Roberto, I don't think there was a ghost in the room," Carol said. "I didn't feel anything strange. Only that cute little white dog and—"

"And that dog's in New York," Roberto argued, "so it must have been Widow Hanson."

Or it could have been, I was thinking, *the ghost of someone else. The ghost of the woman with brown hair. The ghost of the woman whose name began with J.*

Maybe my mother's ghost moved to North Klondike, California. She's not going to open her mouth and speak, she's going to throw things, like hairbrushes and wardrobes and dishes of apple crisp.

But why? Why is she so mad?

9

The Ghosts of Rossetti and Rose

Afterward Roberto and Danny went upstairs to play computer games. Dad, Carol, and I settled on the front porch steps with glasses of organic, herbal, non-caffeinated, pesticide-free iced tea. It tasted okay, if you liked water.

"Professor Barrymore seems nice, even if she is a little strange," Dad said.

"What's so strange about her?" I asked. "Looking for ghosts isn't strange."

"Right," he said. "Looking for ghosts is just as normal as—what?—writing computer software or—"

"Having psychic ability?" Carol said, then smiled at me.

"I don't think she's strange at all," I said. "And there's nothing wrong with looking for ghosts or seeing a ghost either."

"I never said there was."

"Or believing that this house is haunted. Something strange is going on. You've just missed it all, except the apple crisp and you think that was an accident."

"What else could it have been? Dishes of apple crisp just don't go flying through the air."

"Well, you know what happened with the wardrobe and Mom's locket, but I never told you about my hairbrush."

"What?"

"Let me explain," I said and filled him in. "I mean, so many weird things have been happening. It makes sense to me that a ghost might be involved."

Dad's expression changed. I could tell he was thinking something like, *Oh, God, she's at it again with all that ghost stuff.*

"I find that hard to believe," he said. "It doesn't make any sense to me. Christina, you've got to admit that there's no proof."

"I knew you wouldn't agree," I said. "That's what you always say. You think I'm crazy."

"I didn't say that," he replied.

"You didn't have to. I *have* seen a ghost before. And you know it." I looked at Carol and added, "It was my mother's ghost."

"Tell me about it," Carol said.

I told Carol about my mother's ghost and her

locket on the night she died. Dad squirmed the whole time.

"And I saw her more than once. There was another time, when I was older, after Mousie died, but I didn't tell you," I said, looking at him. "I knew you'd just say it was a dream again. The night I buried Mousie—that was my pet mouse who died when I was seven—I looked out my window," I told Carol, "and I saw her ghost standing over Mousie's grave in the back yard. So I've seen her ghost two times, I know it."

"You haven't even seen her ghost once," Dad argued. "The first time was a dream, and the second time you didn't see your mom. I'll agree that you saw someone. But it wasn't her. It was me."

"You were in the back yard looking at Mousie's grave at night?"

"I was thinking."

"I don't believe you."

"All right," he said, sounding very annoyed. "You want a ghost story, I'll give you a ghost story. It starts in a cemetery, and it ends in a cemetery. I've never told it to you before. I never thought I'd have to, but I can see that I don't have a choice now. Just don't tell me later that you can't sleep."

"Ghosts don't scare me," I said. "Whether they're in a cemetery or not."

The First Ghost Story of John Rose

You know I loved your mother very much, and I still do, but there *are* some things I've never told you—like how we met. You know that we met in London, but I never told you where. Actually, it was in a cemetery named Highgate.

Now Highgate is an interesting place. It's very old, and a lot of famous people are buried there. At one time it was beautiful—if you can think of a cemetery as having beauty—but it was neglected over the years. The undergrowth crept over the graves until the place looked more like a forest, and the tombstones began to crumble, and the tombs were damaged by vandals—and then the owners went bankrupt. Some people who loved the place took charge next, but to preserve it they would only open it to the public once or twice a year. That all happened before your mother and I went there.

I was twenty-four and on my first trip to England when I happened to read in the newspaper that Highgate was going to be open on the weekend. I didn't really know anything about it, except that Karl Marx was buried there. I decided to go. I can't say why;

maybe it was fate. Or maybe I was looking for some kind of really English adventure. Cemeteries are a big thing there. But I wasn't looking for ghosts. That's not the kind of thing I'd do. It's more the type of thing that your mother would do. That's why I bumped into her there.

She wasn't exactly like me. She didn't just happen to read that Highgate was going to be open. She had written ahead, gotten all the details, and planned her entire vacation around seeing it. It's on a hill, and people were lined up all the way down to the bottom that day, but your mother was the twenty-seventh person in line. She was looking for the grave of someone very important to her, and she was not going to be disappointed.

Only your mother got lost. She was always terrible at reading maps, and Highgate is such a huge, confusing place. She wandered around, trying to find her bearings. No one seemed able to help her, then she saw me. What was it about me? I don't have any idea. She came right up to me and asked if I could help her find a grave. And since she seemed so nice and was so beautiful and because it seemed like we had known each other for a long time, I deciphered the map and led her to the grave of Christina G-word Rossetti, the poet she named you after.

It's no wonder she couldn't find it. It was off the main lane and down a smaller path overgrown with bushes and weeds. When we found it, your mother was so emotional about seeing it—because she was a very emotional person (kind of like you, and don't get mad)— she began to recite her favorite Christina Rossetti poem, "Remember Me." Only instead of looking at the grave to recite it, she looked right at me. I think I fell in love with her immediately. How could I not?

I know this might sound strange to you, but it wasn't. Somehow Christina Rossetti communicated to your mother, and her poetry was so important to her that she came to Highgate. Somehow we met there and fell in love, standing over the grave of Christina Rossetti. That made Christina Rossetti even more special. So when your mother found out she was having boy and girl B.O.M.A.s—see how many things you've taught me, you little G-word?— she wanted to name them something wonderful. She didn't want anything cute like Robert and Roberta or Jack and Jill. She wanted names that meant something to her. And then she thought of Christina Rossetti, since Rose is like Rossetti, and her brother, Dante.

I know you hate your name, and I know you thought your mother was crazy to call you that. But we couldn't tell you about the cemetery when your mother was alive because— well, how could we? You were too little. It sounded too strange and scary. And when you got older, none of us wanted to talk about what had happened, so I never told you. Dante was an artist and he wrote some poetry, too. It's really funny that Danny likes to draw and that you, Christina, like to write so much. You turned out just the way your mother would have wanted.

"So who threw the apple crisp? The ghosts of Dante and Christina Rossetti?" I asked, thinking this was the stupid kind of ghost story that Dad would tell.

"No," he said.

"Then what's the ghost story?"

"Keep listening."

The night your mother died, you said she came into your room and gave you the Remember Me locket. After that, everything changed. You were such a cute little girl, so beautiful, so happy. And then you changed. I mean, we all changed, but you seemed to change the most. Everything happy went away and all that was left was you and your ghosts.

I don't think you're crazy, but you used to drive me crazy. You used to be a pink-dress girl, remember? With pink tights and pink barrettes, but it seemed like overnight almost, everything changed to black. Or dark green or dark maroon or dark gray. And no dresses, only pants. And then all the games you played. Do you remember playing Names, when you and Danny would pretend to be storybook characters? He would be Prince Charming, and you'd be Snow White's mother. He'd be Cinderella's prince, and you'd pretend to be Cinderella's mother. You were always the ghost. You scared him so much he had to sleep with the lights on. Thank God that's over.

Do you remember what happened when I taught you to read? I thought it would be good for you to know how to read before kindergarten and you seemed interested, so I picked out an Angelina book and taught you how to read it. I knew you had a thing for mice. You thought they were so cute. I thought a cute little ballerina mouse might make you happy again. But the first time you read *Angelina Ballerina* by yourself, you looked at me and asked—I could never forget this—you said, "What would happen if Angelina died? Would she turn into a ghost?"

Everything was *ghosts*. So I got you Mousie. If I thought he was going to die, I wouldn't have done it. But I thought you might have fun taking care of a real mouse. So Mousie died and you wanted to bury him. It bothered me, especially when I saw the locket. We hadn't talked about the locket in years, but somewhere you remembered enough to put it on Mousie.

That night I couldn't sleep and I can't explain it, I don't know why. I went outside and stood by Mousie's grave. I would have driven to the cemetery and stood by your mother's grave if I could have that night. But I had to make do with Mousie's grave.

And you must have seen me. You must have

seen *me* and thought I was your mother's ghost. But how could I have known, because you never told me until now. I wanted so much for you to stop being obsessed with ghosts, especially after that crazy dream of yours, that I gave you your mother's locket. Ghosts, ghosts, ghosts! I feel like I'm going crazy!

Don't get me wrong. I don't blame you for thinking about ghosts. I'd wonder about the hairbrush and the wardrobe and the apple crisp. And I'd wonder why the locket shocked you the first time you touched it. If I was going to believe in ghosts, I'd wonder about these things, too.

I'd wonder why, if your mother was a ghost, she came to see you and not me the night she died. Or why she didn't visit both of us. And what about Danny? Why not him? Or even more than that, I'd wonder if the woman I met in Highgate Cemetery was the ghost of Christina Rossetti. What if I fell in love with a ghost?

But none of this ghost stuff happened. I don't believe in ghosts. I'd give you a million dollars if I could see your mother again, just for a moment, even her ghost, but that's not going happen. I know that when the mother of a little girl and boy dies, it's very upsetting, and nothing ever seems right again. I know that problems come out in dreams. I know that things happen and can seem strange when they're really perfectly normal. Static electricity in a locket, a slippery dish of apple crisp, a wobbly wardrobe, a hairbrush that tips over. They all have perfectly normal explanations.

So this is as close to a ghost story as you'll ever get from me. It started in Highgate, and it ended by Mousie's grave. The only ghost is me. I guess you could say that I am your mother's ghost.

"That's not really a ghost story," I said.

"Sure it is. It's about a ghost. Whether it's real or not is something else."

"You should've told me how worried you were."

"You should've told me you thought you saw Mom's ghost again."

"Sounds like you're both even," Carol said. "Why don't you just promise each other you won't keep any more secrets like these?"

"Good," he said. "Then I can get some more tea. I'll be right back."

When Dad had gone inside, Carol said, "You have a wonderful father, you know."

"I know."

"It's not easy when there's a tragedy," she said. "When someone you love dies. When someone you love is . . . dying."

I looked at her closely.

"Roberto's father, *cara*." She reached over and touched my cheek. "Roberto is so sad, he's so worried, but he tries to keep such a happy face. Maybe you and Danny can help."

"How?" I asked.

"I don't know exactly. Why don't you come by the store tomorrow afternoon? My helper's off for the day. Early afternoon is always slow, so we'll have a chance to talk. Okay?"

"Sure," I said.

We talked a little more, and then I went upstairs. I had to write my ghost reports, but I had to do my computer diary first. I had just turned on my computer when Danny knocked on my door.

"What are you doing?" he asked.

"Just stuff." Danny didn't know anything about my diary and that's the way I was going to keep it. "Where's Roberto?"

"He and Carol went home."

"Come in and shut the door," I said. "I found out some things."

104

"Like what?" he asked, sitting on my bed.

"His father's dying. Carol wants us to help him."

"What's wrong with his dad?"

"I don't know. Do you want to know something else?"

"What?"

I wondered if Dad's "ghost" story was supposed to be a secret, but he hadn't said it was. *Why couldn't Danny know?* I was thinking. So I told him. About how I saw her ghost, except it was really Dad. About how he decided to give me her locket. Danny listened, didn't say much really, and then got up to leave.

"Goodnight," he said, opening the door.

Just then, a picture of my mother fell off the mantel and crashed to the floor.

"Oh, no," I said. The glass had shattered into a spider web shape, but it hadn't sprayed onto the floor. "Is this something weird or is this something normal? I don't understand."

"I don't either," Danny agreed. "Maybe it fell over when I opened the door."

"Maybe, but I don't think so."

As soon as Danny had gone, I sat at my computer and typed:

I DON'T CARE WHAT DAD SAYS; I *AM* BEING HAUNTED BY MY MOTHER'S GHOST!

10

The Investigation Continues

"Is this Christina Rose?" a caller asked when I answered the phone early the next morning.

"Yes."

"Good, it is I."

"Who?"

"I, dear, I. Barrymore. I am calling to invite you and your brother and Roberto to my house for tea this morning. Would ten-thirty be all right?"

"Well, yes, I mean, I guess, for us, but I don't know about Roberto. I can check, he's probably not busy, so—"

"Be a dear girl, Christina," said the professor, "and make sure to bring the reports you completed. I cannot proceed with the investigation unless I've read what you have to say. Toodles."

"T.T.F.N.," I started to say, but she had already hung up the phone.

A while later, Danny and I ran to Roberto's house.

"What's wrong?" Roberto asked, still looking sleepy in his dog-print pajamas.

"The Professor called," I said. "She wants us to take our reports to her house at ten-thirty."

"We're invited for tea," Danny added.

"I don't drink tea," Roberto said.

"Well, you do now," I said. "Why are you still in bed? Do you always sleep this late?"

"No," he said, sounding a little annoyed. "My mom and I had to go out last night—kind of unexpectedly—and I didn't get to bed till four."

"You weren't doing a stakeout, were you?" I asked.

"No."

"Not even with a cow?" I joked.

"What?" Roberto asked sleepily.

"Stakeout, cow, get it?"

"It's too early for puns," he groaned.

"What were you doing?" I asked.

"Mind your own business," Danny said, "and let him get dressed."

Danny pulled me away from Roberto's door and back to our house.

"Why didn't you want to know what he was doing last night? Don't you think that was pretty weird?"

"If he wanted to tell you what he was doing, he would. Just leave him alone."

A few minutes before ten-thirty, a different Roberto was standing at our front door. He was awake, alert, and back to his old sense of humor.

"What do you think her house is going to look like inside?" I asked.

"Like the house in *The Addams Family*," Roberto said. "Cobwebs, dark hallways, and Cousin It hiding in the closet. Just watch out for the crawling hand—or is it hands—they might be visiting from your house!"

"Good! Maybe she'll keep them," I said.

"But what if she's a witch or something?" Danny asked. "What if she tricks kids and traps them in her house?"

"I already told Dad where we're going to be," I said. "He'll rescue us."

A witch didn't answer the door. Professor Barrymore was wearing a white jump suit and white Nikes. Her hair was down and she looked . . . well, she looked perfectly normal and pretty.

"Good work," Professor Barrymore said when we handed her ten ghost reports. I had written five (the shocking locket, the hairbrush, the wardrobe, the apple crisp, and the falling picture); Roberto had written two (the wardrobe and the apple crisp); Dad and Carol had each done one about the apple crisp. Danny had drawn one, and that was it.

"I'll read them later," Professor Barrymore continued. "Right now, I would like to ask each of you some questions about your attic experience privately. Of course, I'll have to tape record it so I don't miss a scintilla of evidence. Roberto, you seem to think that you saw a ghost, so let me follow up on that first. Why don't you have a seat in my office? Christina and Danny, you can amuse yourselves in the living room."

Her house was as far from *The Addams Family* as you could get. The outside may have been a wreck, but the inside was fixed up—and empty. Like the living room: It had one chair and one floor lamp and a stack of what looked like big throw pillows. All of them were placed in the center of the room.

"Where are we supposed to sit?" Danny asked.

"Sit on a pillow," I told him, as I sat in the chair.

Danny started to lift the top pillow from the pile when Professor Barrymore hurried back into the room.

"No, no, dear, not those pillows. Those are a sculpture. You must leave those alone. There's a futon tucked in the front hall closet. Help yourself to that."

Then she left.

Danny looked at me. "What's a futon?"

"I don't know," I said. "Go see what's in the closet."

In a moment he had found a rolled-up mat. "What do you do with this?" he asked. "It looks like something from gym class."

"I think you use it for meditation or something," I said. "Actually it's the kind of thing Sparky would love to sleep on."

"Don't talk about him," Danny said. "I never want to hear about him again."

"Okay," I said.

So Danny and I sat in silence until Roberto came in and took my place.

The office was lined with bookcases from floor to ceiling. Again, the furniture was in the center of the room: one desk and two overstuffed armchairs. An overworked fax machine was grinding away on the floor by the door.

"Don't mind the fax. I'm getting an eighty-odd-page report on a haunting in Australia," Professor Barrymore said. "Now let me pull out your ghost reports and see what we have brewing here in North Klondike."

While she read my reports, I scanned her bookcases. They were full of books about ghosts. I had never seen so many ghosty books.

"My dear," she said, "something seems to be afoot."

"It is," I agreed. "It's my mother's ghost. She's haunting us—well, me, actually. She's haunting me."

"Really," she said. "Tell me why you think so."

So I told her everything about my mother and her locket, and every strange thing that had happened in North Klondike.

"See," I concluded, "it's my mother. It has to be. She's mad that we moved to California."

She jotted a few notes, then looked up at the ceiling, thinking.

"So, it's my mother's ghost, right?"

"Christina, it's too soon to say. I don't like to speak about these things until I have all of the factual evidence. Let me speak to Danny now."

After Danny had his turn, Professor Barrymore boiled some water for tea, made a quick phone call, and then called us into her kitchen.

The table looked as if the Queen of England was scheduled to arrive at any moment. Each place had a china plate and a cloth napkin. Two large plates of sandwiches were in the center.

"Sit down," the Professor said, carrying a tray to the table. On it there were four tea cups and saucers and something large, white, and fuzzy.

"What's that?" Roberto asked.

"My tea cozy," she said. "You put it on the teapot to keep the tea at the proper temperature. Do you like this one? I knitted it myself."

From the back, it looked like a white sweater for her teapot. Then she turned it around. The front had two large black eyes near the top and a large black howling mouth at the bottom, all knitted into the cozy.

"What's it supposed to be?" Roberto asked.

"Is something wrong with your visual acuity? Why, it's a ghost!" she explained. "I call it my ghosty cozy." Then she poured a drop of milk into each tea cup. "It is obvious that the three of you do not know the first thing about ghosts or ghost hunting. And Danny tells me that you've formed a club called Ghost Hunters I.N.K. I find that a highly laudable enterprise, but I'm afraid I must clear up quite a few misconceptions. If you're going to go ghost hunting, you had better know what you're doing or you will find yourself in a spot of bother." She removed the ghosty cozy, filled the cups with tea, and passed one to each of us. "Help yourself to the finger sandwiches. They will stimulate your brain cells and help you stay alert. So eat up and use your brains, children. And listen carefully. If you had been thinking when you were in the attic or dodging apple crisp, you'd have paid more attention to some very important factors. Such as,

"Number one: If there's a ghost in the house, you will see it. A ghost does not make noise, and a ghost does not kill people with furniture. Number two: If you see a ghost, you *will* remember what it looks like. Usually it's someone you know, such as a relative or a close friend."

"You mean, like a mother?" I asked.

"Yes, if the mother is deceased. This is one of the most common kinds of ghosts."

"What about a former neighbor?" Roberto asked. "Like Widow Hanson or her husband."

"Ro-ber-to," she said, in the best Spanish accent, "you have such a wonderful imagination and you may grow up to write screenplays one day if you keep nurturing it as you do, but allow me to dispense with your foolishness once and for all. I have made an inquiry about Widow Hanson and I have found that the so-called ghost story you told me is full of *glaring* inaccuracies. It is true that Widow Hanson's husband left the house quite suddenly, but hardly because he had been carved up by his wife. I spoke to Professor Collinson, who is an expert in the history and folklore of the California coast, and he is well acquainted with the entire Widow Hanson myth—for it is simply a myth. He tells me that her husband left her one day for a woman who lived on a farm outside Castroville. On the woman's farm he had an accident with a combine, and both of his hands were detached. He lived for a number of years after that. The only similarity with Roberto's tale is that he was not buried with his hands, 'tis true, but that is because they were disposed of after his accident and not at the time of his death. Of course, none of this has anything to do with his wife. Widow Hanson, you would have learned, if you had bothered to check the obituaries, died in her sleep at the age of seventy-nine, sitting in her wheelchair at the Gull Haven Nursing Home in Oro del Mar. Your account was imaginative, Roberto, but completely unbelievable. Real ghosts do not behave like that at all."

"But I'm sure I saw her," Roberto protested.

"I am certain that you thought you saw something, but I am equally certain that you did not see Widow Hanson's ghost."

"Forget Widow Hanson," I told Roberto. "What's number three?"

"Number three?" Professor Barrymore asked. "Oh, yes, number three. Number three is very simple; I call it the Most People rule. Most people never become ghosts, and most people never see ghosts. Ghosts are not everywhere, the way many people seem to think they are. Very few people ever become ghosts, but some people seem to think that the living are queuing up, waiting to die and turn into these frightening, foul creatures they've imagined ghosts to be. There are so few ghosts in this world and they are usually much more melancholy than frightening."

"Melancholy?" Roberto asked.

"Sad. Ghosts are so frightfully sad. Have you ever considered that? Which leads to my last thought. Number four: So many people are simply desperate to catch a glimpse of a ghost. So much energy, so much sadness. When I investigate a possible haunting, I always devote more time to determining why the so-called haunted person wants to see a ghost than I do to whether a ghost actually exists.

"Like you, Christina. Why do you want to see a ghost so much? Because you think your mother's ghost is haunting you? If she is, this will explain everything that's happened to you recently. If she is, you think that your father will move you right back to New York. This is actually the part about ghosts that I find truly frightening.

"And you, Danny, I'm not certain that you want to see a ghost at all. Of course, that is interesting in and of itself.

"And Roberto, why are ghosts so important to you that you fabricated a story about Widow Hanson's ghost?"

He shrugged.

"You shouldn't feel at all embarrassed. Even I have concocted a few ghost stories in my time."

"You have?" he asked.

"I'll give you an example."

Professor Barrymore's Second Ghost Story

When my father was ill for a time, I decided that my house in England was haunted. I felt a presence in the house. Mind you, I was twenty years old and well on my way to becoming a parapsychologist and I knew all the pitfalls, but I helped myself believe that my house was haunted. Sudden drafts of cold air gusting around dark corners, odd noises ticking in the cellar, a closet door swinging open. Our house was built in 1702 and it was quite isolated in the Dales, so none of these should have been surprising. But I lost control of my imagination.

One night I was in bed, sleeping soundly, when I was awakened at two o'clock. I was certain that I had heard a noise coming from the W.C.—the toilet, rather—in the upstairs hall. I was certain that I had heard the door close and someone pull the chain to flush the toilet and then bump up against the door, because it was quite a narrow little room, and lift the latch, which made a kind of clicking sound, and open the door. I know it sounds perfectly normal, but my father was gravely ill at the time and I thought at first that he had woken up. Then I heard more sounds as if someone had stumbled in the hall. I thought perhaps he needed help, so I sprang out of bed and rushed to the hall, but of course no one was there.

I peered into my parents' bedroom and they were in bed. My father was snoring loudly, so I deduced that he had not been out of bed. And my mother, who slept on the far side of the bed, appeared to be asleep. But I walked around the bed and looked at her face just to be certain, and she was sleeping soundly as well. No one else was in the house, except me.

I felt my heart rate increase and my vision narrow. A wave of terror swept over me, as I concluded that some ghostly presence—the one I had been aware of for weeks—had used the upstairs toilet.

I asked myself what I should do. I knew I could not sleep a wink that night, so I leapt into the abyss! I pressed pushpins into the baseboards and tied threads around them and strung them to the stairway railings.

I was either going to catch a burglar or watch a ghost pass through the threads. I secreted myself in a dark corner of the hall, by the linen cupboard, and I waited all night for the return of the presence.

As you might suppose, I fell asleep sometime later and was awakened—not by some menacing ghost or ghastly evil presence—but by my mum, who had tangled herself in the threads and almost broken her neck tripping on them. That's how dangerous a ghost hunt can be sometimes.

Of course, you want to know what happened to that toilet-flushing presence that so scared me in the middle of the night, and rightly so. The next morning I discovered my toilet flusher. On my way out of the house to university that day, I was carrying a sack of rubbish for the dustbin—the garbage can, Roberto. I walked out the kitchen door and saw that our dustbin had been turned over and the rubbish scattered about. By dogs, no doubt. It had happened before, and I realized (as soon as I saw it that morning) that it must have happened at two in the morning. It was directly beneath my bedroom window. No matter how certain I was of what my ears had heard, I am convinced that the toilet-flushing ghost was nothing more than a pack of marauding dogs in the dustbin.

It took that silly little experience—quite embarrassing, really—to bring me to my senses and show me the errors I had allowed myself to make.

"But we didn't have a pack of dogs in our attic or in our kitchen," I said. "We saw the wardrobe move and the apple crisp fall on the floor."

"Indeed, Christina, you could have your own dog pack that's responsible for these experiences, because, you see, these two experiences do not add up to a ghost by themselves."

"Then what do they add up to?" I asked.

"I am not saying that you have imagined these things either. Possibilities do exist between ghosts at one extreme and accidents or overly active imaginations on the other."

"Like what?"

"Well, I prefer not to speculate so early in an investigation because that does tend to overstimulate some people's imaginations. However, in this case, I will make a slight exception. As I was saying, it was not a ghost and perhaps it also was not an accident or even your imagination. What I did not say was that it could perhaps be a poltergeist."

"A poltergeist?"

"Widow Hanson's poltergeist!" Roberto exclaimed.

"Widow Hanson is quite dead," Professor Barrymore said.

"Yes, and it's her poltergeist!"

"Absolutely not. You have so much to learn, Roberto. Poltergeists are not ghosts, and they are not the spirits of the deceased. Poltergeists aren't really beings at all, they are simply—and I do not mean to say that it is actually simple, for the phenomenon is quite complex—an energy force that is usually destructive and is associated with a *living* person."

"I don't understand," Roberto said.

"Oh my God, Roberto, don't you get it?" I practically yelled. "I think Professor Barrymore is saying that one of us is causing a poltergeist."

And I was sure I knew exactly who she meant.

11

Christina's Reading

~~~

"Steady on, Christina," Professor Barrymore said. "Before you jump to any further conclusions, let's peruse the circumstantial evidence."

She picked up a paper napkin and a pen from the center of the table and made a chart:

	SHOCKING LOCKET	HAIR-BRUSH	ATTIC WARDROBE	APPLE CRISP	FALLING PICTURE
PERSONS PRESENT					
LOCATION					

"Let's determine who was present at each experience and where each one occurred."

In a moment the chart was complete:

	SHOCKING LOCKET	HAIR-BRUSH	WARDROBE	APPLE CRISP	FALLING PICTURE
PERSONS PRESENT	CR DR JR	CR DR	CR DR RW	CR JR DR CW RW	CR DR
LOCATION	C's Bedrm	C's Bedrm	Attic	Kitchen	C's Bedrm

"Now what do you see?" she asked.

"A lot of initials," Roberto joked.

"I see that I don't want to sleep in my bedroom anymore," I said.

"Not exactly," the Professor said. "Based on this chart alone, I become quite interested in looking more closely at one location—your bedroom, Christina—and two individuals: Danny and Christina. You two were the only ones present at every experience. If I suspect poltergeist activity, I am certainly going to consider each of you, but that does not mean either of you is causing any activity. It could be something else entirely and probably is. I have learned that it is best to suspect the most normal possibility, and poltergeists are hardly that one. Still, I would like to rule it out."

"How can you do that?" Roberto asked.

"By exploring it scientifically. First we need to add one more line to our chart, like so:

	SHOCKING LOCKET	HAIR-BRUSH	ATTIC WARDROBE	APPLE CRISP	FALLING PICTURE
PERSONS PRESENT	CR DR JR	CR DR	CR DR RW	CR JR DR CW RW	CR DR
LOCATION	C's Bedrm	C's Bedrm	Attic	Kitchen	C's Bedrm
ACTIVITY DIRECTLY PRECEDING					

"It's important to determine what was happening right before each experience. By this I mean what you were doing, what you were saying, even what you were thinking if it seems at all relevant. Oh, dear, look at the time. Christina, why don't you take this chart with you and think about this today?" she said, handing it to me. Then she started to clear the table, all the while talking to us. "Perhaps the three of you can put your heads together before we meet again. Jot down some thoughts, would you, dears? Drop them in my mailbox by sixish. That should allow me some time to comb your ghost reports for any important clues and plan my experiment, which of course we will want to conduct in your bedroom. Do you think your father will mind?"

"I don't think so," I said.

"Good. But I must go to work now. I have classes to teach. What if I come over this evening about eight? I can bring my equipment and get started. The experiment shouldn't take long."

"Toodles," we said and headed for the door.

"A ghost hunt at eight," Roberto said as we walked down Professor Barrymore's front walk. "This is awesome!"

"Not a ghost hunt," I said. "An experiment in search of a poltergeist."

"It's a ghost hunt," Roberto repeated.

"Let's work on the chart," I suggested.

"No way," Danny said. "Let's do something else."

"Like what?" Roberto asked.

"Come on, you two. You were supposed to help with the chart."

"We don't need to do the chart. I already know what's going to happen," Roberto said. "Widow Hanson's ghost is going to make her appearance. Just wait. Or her husband's hands are going to come crawling down your hallway. I'm bringing my camera."

"That's enough," I said.

"Get your bike and some quarters," Roberto said to Danny. "I'll come to get you in five minutes. We can go to the Klondike Shell Station and play video games."

A minute later, I was in the kitchen drinking a glass of seltzer when Dad walked in.

"Okay," he said, "do you want the good news or the bad news about school?"

"Danny," I yelled. "Get down here."

If there was bad news, I wanted company.

In a second Danny walked in, stuffing quarters into his jeans pocket.

"What?" he asked.

"Bad news about school," I said.

"First the good news," Dad told us. "The classes

are really small at North Klondike Elementary, so you'll get a lot of attention from the teacher."

"But?" I prompted.

Dad nodded. "But there's only one class at each grade level, so the two of you will be together." Then he added quickly, "It isn't really bad news, if you're to—"

Danny exploded like a rocket. "Together? With her? I don't want to be with her. She's so bossy!"

"Well, thanks a lot," I said. "You're no thrill either."

"Kids, come on. Roberto will be with you. It won't be so bad."

"We haven't been together since nursery school," Danny explained. "Why did we have to move to this stupid place?"

"It'll be okay," Dad said. "I'll talk to the teacher. You can sit on different sides of the room. You won't have to do any projects together. You can have separate friends, separate everything. You don't even have to walk to school together. We'll work out all your clothes ahead of time so you never both show up wearing the same color or anything." Dad grinned.

"I don't wear black," Danny said.

"Well, I don't wipe dirt all over my clothes," I countered.

"I'll be sure to buy you different pens and pencils and notebooks, so no one will think that you're trying to be twi— I mean, B.O.M.A.s. You can tell everyone that you're just two homeless kids that I picked up off some subway grate in New York City and brought home and you have no genetic similarities at all—except, of course, your nasty tempers! Work it out, guys," Dad said. "I'll help you any way I can, but I can't take a fight right now."

He left the room.

I looked at Danny. He looked at me.

"You're such a jerk sometimes," I said.

"And you're not?" he asked.

Just then Roberto knocked on the back door.

"Go rot your brain with video games," I said. "I have someplace better to go."

I grabbed my sunglasses and headed for the door. I wanted to elbow him when I passed by, but I didn't. Things were bad enough as they were.

"Hi, you're early," Carol said.

"Too early?" I asked. The store was totally empty of people.

"Not today. Business is slow. But wait till the week before school starts. Everyone will be back then."

"Wow!" I said, looking around. Carol's Klondike Krystal Palace was stuffed, floor to ceiling.

"Do you want a tour?"

"Sure."

She walked me down the three narrow aisles. They

were divided into little sections. Little kids' toys, art supplies, incense and body oils, New Age books, hair stuff, New Age music, candles, beads, earrings, wind chimes, Halloween masks, Mexican coconut masks, piñatas, and so much more stuff I can't even remember. Except the last and biggest section: CANDY!

"I really wanted to start a book store, but North Klondike isn't exactly the place to do that. Most of the town doesn't even care that the library's only open one day a week. So I had to diversify. A few books, a little this, a little that. And the candy and the Snapple and the ice cream and my baked goodies. That's where I make my money. But only when the kids are around after school. Want a muffin? They're orange cranberry and I just made them this morning."

"Not really," I said.

"What's wrong?"

"I had to get out of the house," I said. "Boys—and dads—can drive me crazy."

"What'd they do?"

"Danny's having a fit that we have to be in the same class at school. What am I? Poison or something? What's he afraid of? That I'm going to steal all his friends? Or do better on my homework? Or give away all his deep dark secrets?"

"Well, all those sound like good reasons to me," Carol said.

"This is such a *twin* thing. I hate being a twin! God, it's like having permanent cooties!"

"One day it might not seem so bad."

"Yeah, like the day I die."

"Since you have to be in the same class, maybe you can find a way to let him know that you won't crowd him."

"Yeah, like dip myself in a vat of vanishing cream."

"Oh, Christina, you'll find a way." Then she yawned. "Sorry, we were up half the night."

"Why?"

"A friend called and told us that Roberto's father was dying right then, and that we'd better get there. So we jumped in the car around midnight and we headed up to San Jose. Thank God I have a car phone. They called from the hospital to say that he was doing better and that we didn't need to come. We still had two hours to drive, so I turned around and came home. I think we crawled into bed at about four. We're both pretty tired today. I wouldn't even have come into work, but my helper has today off. This is the third time this month his father has made an emergency run to the hospital, and they've all been at night. It's getting to the point that I'm think- ing about saying no, we're not going, I don't care if he's dying."

"You can't do that."

"And why not?"

"Because . . . because . . ." *Why?* I was asking myself. And I knew: "Because you'll never see him again."

"Like your mother?" Carol asked.

It was weird. Maybe it was just because I was so mad at Danny or all this ghost stuff or I don't know what. But Carol looked at me in such a crystal clear way that she could see everything inside me. At least it felt that way. My eyes started filling with tears.

"God, I hate myself when I do that," I said, wiping the tears away. "I hate me, I hate me."

"Why? Because you miss your mother?"

I shrugged. "Because of everything. Because I think her ghost is haunting me and then Professor Barrymore tells me I'm wrong and now—this is really crazy—I think I'm a poltergeist. God, next I'll turn into a witch. Danny already thinks I am one."

Carol put an arm around me and squeezed. "Calm down," she said. "You're going to be fine. Now why in the world do you think you're a poltergeist?"

So I told her what Professor Barrymore had said and what had happened to the picture frame.

"Christina, it could have just fallen over when Danny opened the door. Maybe there was some air movement, you know how wobbly picture frames can be sometimes. If it'll make you feel any better, I owe you a reading, but maybe a little different kind. Are you wearing your mother's locket?"

"Yes."

"Anything else that belonged to your mother?"

"These sunglasses."

"Great," she said. "Let's sit over here." We parked ourselves on chairs behind the cash register. It was very strange. Carol had a Yanni tape on the sound system, incense was burning by the Krystal Korner (which had a glass display case full of crystal pendants and earrings), and three votive candles in stained glass holders were speckling the room with colors. *This could only happen in California*, I was thinking.

Carol took the sunglasses and said, "Sometimes I can hold an object and get feelings from it. I don't know if that can help you with this poltergeist idea or not. But it doesn't hurt to try—as long as you don't mind. Okay?"

"Okay," I said.

She held the sunglasses lightly in her hands and closed her eyes. As she sat there quietly, her fingers began to trace the frames.

"It seems to come from a young woman. It seems to come from brown hair, long brown hair, and green eyes. Definitely green eyes."

I sat there with my mouth open, only Carol wasn't looking at me. She was describing my mother.

"And a blue car with two car seats and something hanging. It seems to come from two dolls hanging from the mirror."

"Oh my God," I said. "I forgot about that. Thing One and Thing Two."

"Shh!" Carol said, her eyes still closed. "Let me finish. It seems to come from two children, toddlers, smiling up at her, seeing their reflections in the lenses. It seems to come from happiness."

She opened her eyes and looked at me.

"That's all, I'm afraid. What about the dolls?"

"Our favorite book was *The Cat in the Hat*, and we loved Thing One and Thing Two—you know, those two naughty things that mess up the house when the mother's away?" Carol nodded. "Danny and I would mess things up sometimes and she'd call us Thing One and Thing Two. We'd all laugh. She liked to sew a little and one day she made us our own Thing One and Thing Two. We loved them and we always wanted to take them out with us, but we were always dropping them or losing them for a while, so Mom hung them from the rear-view mirror. We called them 'those naughty things' and we made them stay there. Danny and I loved it. How did you know?"

"I don't know. Maybe because she wore her sunglasses in the car. Maybe it was a special feeling for her, too. I just don't know how. But I want to tell you one more thing. I don't feel her around here. I don't feel her presence exactly. I don't think her ghost is here. But let me see the necklace."

I took the sunglasses and handed her the locket.

"Strange," she said, after a few moments. "It seems to come from nothing. I see your father, I see you. But it seems to come from a place where your mother never was. Are you sure this was hers?"

"That's what Dad said," I replied. "You don't think he lied, do you?"

"I wouldn't think so," Carol said. "But listen to me. I don't see any presence around here. Does that make you feel better? I don't know what's happening, but I don't think it revolves around you."

"Then who? Danny?" I asked. "I don't think so."

"I have an idea," Carol said. "Why don't you go home and try to make up with Danny and work things out about school? I bet that would make both of you feel better. And take this box of sandalwood incense. It comes in little cones. Just light the point of the cone. Burn some while you're talking to him and it'll calm you both down. It has such a mellow scent. Oh, and take this," she said, handing me a little piece of pottery. "It's an Egyptian incense holder."

I thanked her for everything and took off for home.

12

The California Poltergeist
————~~~————

At home I found a note from Dad tacked on my bedroom door:

> Try to remember this (please):
>
> There is no friend like a sister (or a brother)
> In calm or stormy weather;
> To cheer one on the tedious way,
> To fetch one if one goes astray,
> To lift one if one totters down,
> To strengthen while one stands.
>
> An extra friend might come in handy next year.
> Love, Dad

Sometimes Dad could be psychic himself. I lit the incense and waited till my bedroom was full of sandalwood smell. Then I called Danny.

"We need to talk," I said as he walked in. "Did Dad put a poem on your door?"

"Yes."

"He put it on my door, too. So let's get this over with. I don't want to fight about school. I won't get in your face. I won't tell any family secrets. I won't open my big mouth about anything. I won't be the evil T-word. I promise."

"I still don't like it," he said.

"Neither do I, but I'm not repeating fifth grade just so you can have a good year without me. I'll make friends with the girls, you'll make friends with the boys. We don't have to have anything to do with each other."

"Fine," he agreed.

The rest of the afternoon I worked on Professor Barrymore's chart. Right before dinner I dropped it into her mailbox. Then I headed home. I had something I wanted to ask Dad.

"I went to see Carol's store today. It's great. Lots of candy and stuff. And she did a reading for me."

"What kind of reading?" he asked.

"She took Mom's sunglasses and told me about Mom. The color of her hair and eyes, and she saw Thing One and Thing Two. Remember? We used to have them hanging from the rear-view mirror in the blue car? Carol saw those."

"I forgot all about them," Dad said.

"Me too," I said. "But then I gave her the Remember Me locket and she couldn't see anything. She wondered if it was really Mom's locket."

"What do you mean?" he asked, sounding annoyed. "Why wouldn't it be?"

"I don't know. Carol just wondered."

"Well, your mother only had it a few hours. Maybe that's why."

"Don't get mad. Carol said to ask you, that's all."

"Do we have to talk about this?" Danny said.

Everyone sat in silence, picking at their dinners. It was one of Dad's best summer meals: salad with roast chicken and his very own low-fat dressing.

Then Dad slammed down his fork and started, "Why did we have to move here? Why did we have to move here? That's all the two of you have been saying. Well, maybe we moved here to set me straight. I made some mistakes, okay. I wasn't the best father, I'll admit, but I've tried hard. And now you're all a bunch of psychics! Okay, I guess I have no choice. You want to know about the locket? I'll tell you about it, but don't say I didn't warn you."

"It's not Mom's locket?"

"No, it's not."

The Second Ghost Story of John Rose

The morning that I told you your mother had died, I couldn't believe you had her locket, but I didn't want to scare you or upset you or make you think about ghosts, so I took the locket away. It should have been with her on the plane. I don't know how it fell into your pocket, but it should have been with her. And so I made sure it was.

I did something stupid. Right before your mother was buried, I had the funeral director put the locket in the coffin with her. I never told anyone—not even Grandma and Grandpa—what I had done. I wanted it to be with her forever. I wanted it to be my secret.

But after she was buried, you started having dreams. You won't remember them now, because you didn't even remember them the next morning. I'd hear you crying in your sleep, screaming sometimes, but you were never really awake. Maybe you were in a trance, I don't know. I never wanted to tell you about these dreams because I thought they'd bother you. But I guess you're old enough now to know.

Every night for a week after your mother was buried you woke up crying. You'd say

"Momma, I want the locket. I want the locket, Momma." Every night I heard you, and I wished I had the locket to give you to get you back to sleep, to stop you from crying. I was feeling so overwhelmed by your mother's death and all the responsibility of taking care of you and Danny.

I knew right away it had been a mistake to bury the locket, but what was I going to do? You didn't know what I had done with it. And I was hardly going to confess and tell you the truth. You never even asked about it when you were awake. But it was all coming out at night. Then, just when I thought it was going to drive me permanently crazy, the dreams stopped, you stopped waking up, and I thought it was all over. So I forgot about it— or maybe I just wouldn't let myself think about it—until Mousie died.

I don't know why or how you got the idea to make that locket out of aluminum foil and bury Mousie with it. But when you showed me what you had done, it bothered me, *really* bothered me. I mean, it was a little disconcerting—and okay, a little spooky—how you seemed to know what I had done. I started to remember all the times you screamed about the locket, and I started going crazy. I felt guilty and stupid and wrong. I had messed everything up. I had ruined your life. It was as if your mother was talking to you and to me, and I knew what I had to do. What if you wanted the locket when you got older? How was I going to explain it?

So that night I waited until you and Danny were asleep—I thought—and then I went outside and just stood by Mousie's grave, thinking. That's when you saw me, I guess. I was thinking about getting the locket back. I needed to think what to do about your mother. How would it feel if I was to get your mother's locket back? Would it bother me? Would it be terrible to do? It didn't seem to be such a bad thing.

So I went through all the paperwork and had your mother's grave opened and the locket removed. I wasn't there to see it, I didn't want to be there, but they took the locket out and gave it to me.

Don't look at me like that, Christina. Just listen. Somehow water had gotten in. It's not supposed to, but it did, and the locket had tarnished. The hinges had rusted. I guess it wasn't sterling silver. It didn't look new anymore. It looked like a piece of junk. So I put it away.

Then after I got the job and you dreamed about the locket again, I thought it wasn't nice enough to give you anymore. I knew if I gave you the real one you'd ask how it got that way. And I thought it would upset you. So I went to the jewelry store and bought another one, only it's not quite the same. That's the one I gave you. The new one. So Carol was right. It didn't belong to your mom.

I guess I have to give you the real one. I guess that's why everything's happening. I am making everyone so unhappy. I can't seem to do anything right.

"Where is the real locket?" I asked.

"Upstairs," he said. "Put away."

"Can I have it?"

"It doesn't bother you? Where it's been?"

"No. Only—where was it? I mean—"

"She wasn't wearing it, if that's what you mean. It was tucked into the side of the—"

"Okay," I said.

"Does that bother you?"

"No."

"You'd tell me if it did, right?"

"Yes."

"I'll get it after dinner," he said.

"May I be excused?" Danny asked. I had forgotten all about him sitting there. "I don't feel hungry."

"Sure," Dad said. "I don't feel hungry either."

I was wearing the real locket when Professor Barrymore rang our doorbell that night at eight-thirty sharp. It was raining, and she was carrying an umbrella to protect her floral bag. I could see rolls of masking tape sticking out, but nothing else.

We were all waiting for her. Carol and Roberto had come over. Roberto brought two backpacks full of poltergeist-hunting equipment, and Carol was going to show Dad how to install a dishwasher. Dad definitely thought it was weird, but he didn't try to stop us. Especially after everything that had been happening.

"Have fun," Dad said.

"Onward!" Professor Barrymore said, and we headed for my room.

"The first thing I must do," she said, "is make a thorough search of your room. You all must stay in the hallway right here."

We watched as Professor Barrymore looked under my bed and in my closet. She tapped on walls and even the closet ceiling. Then she pulled out her masking tape and taped around the window frames.

"I see I won't have to tape these holes up," she said, indicating the cardboard covered windowpanes. Then she put an index card under the leg of each piece of furniture, taped it to the floor, and traced an outline of the shape.

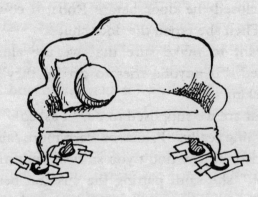

"Why are you doing that?" Roberto asked.

"To see if the furniture moves."

"Do you want some flour?" he asked.

"I am *not* baking a cake," she said, joining us in the hall. "Now we're ready."

"I'm ready, too," Roberto said, taking out a camera. "If anything floats through the door, I'll take its picture."

"Remember, Roberto, poltergeists don't float, so please put your camera away," Professor Barrymore instructed. "Now, dears, here's the plan. Danny and Christina, you're to come inside the bedroom with me and we'll shut the door. Roberto, you'll stay out here in the hall. Once the door is closed, duckie, I want you to stand on this chair and tape all the way round where the door meets the frame. Seal it tightly. I'll tape the inside all the way round as well. Then we'll see what we'll see. T.T.F.N.!"

She closed the door before Roberto could say a word. Then she taped the door shut.

"I want to make sure that we are alone," she explained. "If anyone tries to get in, they'll rip up the masking tape."

"What are we supposed to do?" I asked.

"Nothing really," Professor Barrymore said.

"Christina, why don't you sit here with me on the loveseat," she said, patting the cushion beside her. "And Danny, you can sit on Christina's desk chair."

"Then what?" Danny asked.

"Then you can listen to me," the Professor said. "I'll be sitting right here, in case something happens."

"Is this going to take a long time?" Danny asked.

"One never knows. Now, Christina, I'd like you to take off your locket, please, and hold it in your right hand."

"This isn't the same locket as before," I said. Then I explained what had happened.

"Interesting," the Professor said.

"Which locket do you want me to hold?" I asked. "This one or the other one? I have the first one in my pocket."

"Let me see them, dear." She held both of them a moment, inspecting each one carefully. As she studied them, I could hear the sound of the rain tapping on the window directly in back of the loveseat. And in the distance I could hear the low rumble of thunder.

"Use this one," she said, folding my hand around one of the lockets. She put the other in her purse. I couldn't tell which one she had given me. "Now I want you to tell me what was happening when you first got the shock you described."

"Well, my dad just gave me the locket and it shocked me when I touched it and I dropped it."

"What was he saying to you when he handed you the locket? Can you remember?"

"He was talking about the locket and something like it was a new day in my life and a special memory."

"By special memory, what do you suppose he meant?"

"He meant my mother."

The locket started to feel warm.

"Professor Barrymore, it's getting warm."

"The locket?"

"Yes. What should I do?"

"Nothing. Just hold it, unless it starts to hurt. Now, go on, dear, and tell me about the next time, when the hairbrush flipped, as you describe it."

"We were here, in my bedroom, and Danny and I

were talking. Dad was making pancakes downstairs, and I was trying to hurry so I could get down there."

"What were you saying?"

"Danny seemed kind of lonely and I said something about Sparky, our dog, and then I guess the hairbrush just—it's getting hotter."

"And what about the attic, Christina? What happened there?"

"Roberto threw pebbles and a suitcase slid off some newspapers, and we were getting kind of spooked. Then the wardrobe started moving."

"Did anything happen before the wardrobe moved?"

"No, I don't—well, we found an old rawhide of Sparky's, but—"

"Is it Sparky? Is that the problem?" the Professor asked.

"What do you mean?" I asked.

"Shh, Christina," the Professor said.

"But—"

"Is that what's bothering you, Danny?"

I looked at Danny.

"Is it that Sparky's back in New York?" she asked. "Is that troubling you?"

Suddenly a crash of thunder rocked the house and lightning flashed. The windows in my room began to shake like we were in the middle of a huge tornado.

"This isn't going to bring Sparky here," the Professor said loudly.

The window frames rattled, and the glass panes shook.

"You'll have to ask your father to get Sparky here," Professor Barrymore continued. "He'll do that, Danny, I'm sure he will. All you have to do is ask him. How does the locket feel now, Christina?"

Just then my bedroom lights went out, and a strange noise filled the room. A funny humming noise.

"Don't be afraid, you two," the Professor said. In a second she had turned on a flashlight and held it to her face. "What about the locket, Christina?"

"It's still hot," I said.

Suddenly the Professor's flashlight flew from her hand. It hit the far wall and dropped to the floor, its light bulb shattered.

We were sitting in total darkness again. I was waiting to hear the Professor's voice. Then the humming seemed to get louder, and the loveseat started to vibrate.

"Sit still, Christina. Don't move. No one's going to get hurt."

Then I grabbed her hand and held on tightly.

The humming turned into the buzz of a lawn-mower, then into the steely whine of an engine.

The loveseat was vibrating so much that it seemed to lift off the floor. I couldn't see for sure until the lightning flashed again. The loveseat seemed to have risen a foot into the air. It dipped to the left, steadied itself, and then swung to the right. All the time the engine screeched in my ears.

I knew what was happening. It wasn't just an engine. It was a jet engine. I had the sickening feeling that I was on the plane my mother flew to Maine.

The loveseat dipped again, and my stomach lurched.

"We're going to crash!" I screamed and squeezed Professor Barrymore's hand more. Now the locket was burning my hand.

"It hurts," I said. "The locket hurts."

"Let go of it," the Professor said.

I tried, but the locket seemed to be fighting me. I let go of Professor Barrymore's hand and, using all my strength, lifted the locket above my head, fighting some force that tried to keep me from moving, and flung it on the floor.

Without warning, the windows stopped shaking and the loveseat settled back on the floor. But the engine noise was still blaring.

Then the lights clicked on. Professor Barrymore was standing at the door. Danny was still on the desk chair.

"Are you both all right?" she asked.

"I want Sparky," he said.

"We'll make Dad bring him here," I told him.

"Yes," he said. "Right now."

He stood up, and I started to get up, too. Only I realized that my alarm clock was buzzing. The humming, whining engine was nothing more than the alarm.

I walked to my nightstand and turned off the alarm.

"That's weird," I said, "the alarm wasn't supposed to go off now. I thought the noise was the airplane."

"What airplane?" Professor Barrymore asked.

"Didn't you hear the noise?"

"I heard the alarm, dear. Is that what you mean?"

"No, it didn't sound like an alarm. It sounded like an airplane. I thought it was going to crash."

"Crash?" the professor asked.

"When I was sitting with you on the loveseat. Didn't you feel it go up in the air, like it was flying? Like it was going to crash?"

"Look at the index cards, dear. Did the loveseat move?"

I inspected the loveseat's legs. Each was resting within the shape of the outlines Professor Barrymore had made.

"No, but—"

"Sometimes our imaginations can truly be ruled by our senses, especially when we are thrust into darkness. Darkness can be frightening."

"Well, I wasn't really scared most of the time. You were sitting next to me. And then when I thought the plane was going to crash, I held your hand."

"You did what, dear?"

"I held your hand."

"Really?"

"Weren't you holding my hand?" I asked.

"No, dear," she said. "Why?"

"Someone was holding my hand."

"Oh, dear," the Professor said. "Where's the locket, Christina?"

"I threw it. Or tried to." It was lying on the floor near the foot of my bed. I must have thrown it hard, because now it was broken into two halves. There were two Remember Me's; they were no longer connected. I picked up the locket and showed her. I could see that it was the new locket that had never belonged to Mom.

"Why don't you give one half to Danny?" the Professor suggested. "I think it would make him very happy."

Danny nodded slightly, so I handed him one half of the locket.

"Thank you," he said.

"But it's not the locket Danny wants," I said. "That's the new one. I think he'd rather have half of the real one. We'll have to split it, only it's rusted."

"Perhaps you can take it to a jewelry store tomorrow," Professor Barrymore suggested. "Then Danny will have what he wants."

"Am I the poltergeist?" Danny asked.

"I believe that you were somehow causing the poltergeist activity," Professor Barrymore said. "But you aren't a poltergeist. You're upset about some things. And once those things get taken care of, everything should return to normal. Whatever normal is."

"But whose hand was I holding?"

"I see that I've broken all of my rules," Professor Barrymore said next. "That's what happens when one takes a personal interest in a case. We've ruined our ghost reports, I'm afraid."

"Can we go downstairs now?" Danny asked.

"Yes, I should think we have quite a few things to discuss with your father. But I'd like to ask you a few questions first. Christina, be a dear and run on ahead."

I quickly pulled the tape off my door frame, glad that everything seemed to be okay. Danny was the California Poltergeist, and everything was going to be okay. Then I opened the door and saw that the hallway was dark. Too dark. Roberto was gone.

"That's weird," I said out loud.

I started to walk down the hall toward the stairs. But just before I got to the attic door, it swung open and out stepped the ghost of Widow Hanson.

I was frozen with fear. She had an evil look on her face and bloodshot eyeballs and she was staring right at me.

I screamed in terror.

All of a sudden she turned and started to walk down the hall away from me. My eyes bugged out. Plastered on her back were two bloody dripping handprints.

I couldn't stop myself.

I screamed again.

13

The Very Last Ghost Story—NOT!

——✦——

All right, all right, it was just Roberto standing there in a white sheet and a mask from the Klondike Krystal Palace and ketchup hands on his back. I saw his Reeboks right away and knew it wasn't Widow Hanson.

And, okay, that part about holding one of the hands of Hans was all Roberto's idea. Roberto said I had to put one more fake ghost in, just to make everyone happy, so there you are. Are you *happy?* It was just to keep you on your toes (or should I say, fingers?).

But, I SWEAR, *everything else* was true!

We went downstairs and talked to Dad and Carol. Then Danny and Professor Barrymore came downstairs and we talked some more. Before we knew it, Dad had telephoned Grandma and Grandpa and told them we needed Sparky.

"I don't care what it costs," Dad said. "I want Sparky out here. Danny misses him too much. See if you can get him on a plane tomorrow. Have him sent to L.A. nonstop, and we'll drive down to pick him up."

Grandma and Grandpa called back half an hour later. They had talked to the vet, who didn't recommend sending Sparky as checked baggage because he was too old. Instead the vet thought Sparky would be all right in a small dog carrier tucked under the seat. But that meant we would have to fly to New York to get him.

"They have two frequent flyer tickets they'll use for you and Christina to go get Sparky," Dad told Danny, holding his hand over the telephone mouthpiece. "Okay?"

"Sure," Danny said.

Then he looked at me.

"Okay, Christina? Will you fly there with Danny and bring Sparky home?"

"Why not you?"

"I have to start work," he said. "I wouldn't let Danny go by himself, but I'll let the two of you go together."

"You'll be fine," Carol said.

"And if not, I can always be a ghost, right?" I said.

"I wouldn't worry about that, dear," Professor Barrymore said.

"All right," I said. "I'll do it. Just don't give me any presents before we leave, you *have* to promise."

There were no presents, there were no thunderstorms, there were no crashes. Sparky came to live with us, Roberto's father didn't die, Carol had us over for a scrumptious high-fat dinner. And we took the Remember Me locket to a jewelry store in Oro del Mar to be divided.

Then Professor Barrymore suggested that I write my very own ghost book. Roberto decided to write one, too: *The Widow and Hans Hanson Joke Book.* He told me I could give one example, but you aren't allowed to steal it.

Q: What did Widow Hanson say to the nasty nurse at the Gull Haven Nursing Home?

A: Wait till I get my Hans on you!*

So that's just about the end of my ghost book. Oh, I know what some stupid ghost story writers would do. They'd try to turn my book into a *fake scary* ghost book. They'd hide a battery inside it and just as you

---

*If his book is ever going to appear at your local neighborhood bookstore, Roberto promises to let you know.

get to the last page, the book would go flying out of your hands. Or they'd use a little more imagination and have a wispy white hologram ghost float up from the last page (like they do at Disneyland) and smile a sickening smile, with both its gooey green eyeballs hanging out, and give you the permanent creeps.

But that's not what happens at the end of my ghost book. I just have one more story to tell.

Two days before school began, Dad called Danny and me inside one afternoon and told us this story:

The Third Ghost Story of John Rose

I got the mail this morning and in it there was a large envelope from the agency that investigated the plane crash. I'd gotten some things from them over the years. Your mother's purse, her shoes—you know, those kinds of things. Things you don't want. Things you want to forget.

Anyway, in the envelope was a notebook and a letter. The letter said that recently they were going through some unidentified material associated with the crash, and they were finally able to identify this notebook as belonging to your mother, and they sent it on to us.

It's not much to look at. It obviously got rained on and the pages got warped, and the lines ran a little. If you look through the notebook, it's empty. There's nothing written in it. Your mother always liked to carry a notebook, to write things in. She loved to write. I don't remember, but I guess she bought a new notebook for her trip. That's why nothing was in it yet.

The reason why they know it was hers now is this: it was a three-subject notebook and the dividers each have a pocket. Inside one of the pockets was a postcard your mother had written on the plane, before, you know, and this time someone found the postcard with our Larchmont address and figured the notebook had belonged to her and sent it to me and it got forwarded here.

The postcard is here. See? The Statue of Liberty. It's funny, she must have bought it before her trip. Except she found a picture of Thing One and Thing Two somewhere and glued them on the front. She wanted this postcard to be something special. Do you remember?

Sometimes she called you the Twin Things when you were both giving her a hard time. Of course, she didn't know not to use the T-word because you hadn't yelled at her yet. Anyway, let me read what it says:

Dear Thing One and Thing Two:

I'm in the air now, thinking about you two. You won't get this until after I get home, but I want you to know how special the locket is. I am looking at it right now. It is shiny and bright, just like the two of you. I love you all and I miss you,

Mom XXXOOO

I don't know if she was really looking at the locket. I mean, I guess she could have been *saying* that she was looking at the locket when she really wasn't. She might have realized she had lost it but didn't want to upset you. But maybe, somehow, Christina, you were right about what happened that night. Maybe she was looking at it. Maybe she was wearing it. Maybe she did give it to you. It's hard to understand a lot of things, but maybe this time the message is getting through to me.

"So who wants the notebook and who wants the postcard? How do I divide them up?"

"I don't care," I said. "Danny can pick first."

Danny looked at both of them, then said, "The

postcard." Dad handed it to him. "You inherit the notebook," he told me.

"I want to put this in a frame," Danny said.

"Definitely," Dad answered.

I thought about giving Mom's locket to Carol and asking for another reading, but that's one story (ghost or otherwise) I'm not ready to finish yet. Maybe one day I will.

For now I'm out of ghost stories. But if I've learned one thing, it's that you never know when a ghost is around (if you look for *real* ones). That's why tomorrow, on the first day of school, Roberto and Danny and I are putting signs up on the bulletin boards:

GHOST HUNTERS I.N.K.
WE INVESTIGATE ALL HAUNTINGS
TRAINED BY PROFESSIONAL PARAPSYCHOLOGIST

Under that we list our ghost-hunting phone number (Dad will be *so* happy).

I don't know how many ghosts we're going to discover in this town, but North Klondike seems to be as good a place as any to find them.

But, then, hey, what else would you expect in California?

'Good-bye in fear, good-bye in sorrow,
  Good-bye, and all in vain.
Never to meet again, my dear'—
  'Never to part again.'
'Good-bye today, good-bye tomorrow,
  Good-bye till earth shall wane,
  Never to meet again, my dear'—
    'Never to part again.'

—Christina G-word Rossetti